THE *ROOFTOP* *ADVENTURE* OF *MINNIE AND TESSA,*

FACTORY FIRE SURVIVORS

BY **HOLLY LITTLEFIELD**
ADAPTATION BY **AMANDA DOERING TOURVILLE**
ILLUSTRATED BY **TED HAMMOND** AND **RICHARD PIMENTEL CARBAJAL**

Graphic Universe™ Minneapolis • New York

INTRODUCTION

IN THE EARLY 1900S, NEW YORK CITY HAD MORE CLOTHING FACTORIES THAN ANY OTHER PLACE IN THE WORLD. THE PEOPLE EMPLOYED IN THESE FACTORIES WORKED LONG HOURS FOR LITTLE MONEY. SOMETIMES THEY WORKED MORE THAN 10 HOURS A DAY, SEVEN DAYS A WEEK. MANY OF THESE WORKERS WERE RECENT IMMIGRANTS. THE ONLY JOBS THEY COULD FIND WERE IN THE FACTORIES. IF THEY DIDN'T WORK, THEIR FAMILIES WOULD HAVE NO MONEY TO PAY FOR FOOD, CLOTHES, OR HOUSING.

FACTORY CONDITIONS WERE UNPLEASANT AND OFTEN VERY DANGEROUS. IN THOSE DAYS, FEW LAWS REQUIRED SAFE WORKING CONDITIONS. THE FACTORIES WERE CROWDED AND DIRTY, WITH POOR LIGHTING AND LITTLE AIRFLOW.

THE TRIANGLE SHIRTWAIST COMPANY WAS LOCATED ON THE UPPER FLOORS OF THE ASCH BUILDING IN NEW YORK CITY. MORE THAN 600 PEOPLE—MOSTLY IMMIGRANT WOMEN AND GIRLS FROM EASTERN EUROPE, RUSSIA, AND ITALY—WORKED THERE. THEY MADE FANCY

WOMEN'S BLOUSES CALLED SHIRTWAISTS. THE BLOUSES WERE MADE FROM VERY THIN COTTON OR LINEN FABRIC. THIS MATERIAL WAS DELICATE. IT BURNED MORE EASILY THAN PAPER. THE OWNERS OF THE FACTORY PAID LITTLE ATTENTION TO FIRE SAFETY. CONTAINERS OF SEWING MACHINE OIL WERE KEPT NEAR LARGE BINS OF FABRIC SCRAPS. HIGHLY FLAMMABLE PATTERNS HUNG FROM WIRES ON THE CEILING, AND WORKERS WERE ALLOWED TO SMOKE NEARBY. THE ONE FIRE ESCAPE IN THE BUILDING WAS OLD, DANGEROUSLY STEEP, AND STOPPED TWO FLOORS ABOVE THE GROUND. BUT DESPITE REPEATED COMPLAINTS FROM THE WORKERS, INSPECTORS ALWAYS APPROVED THE BUILDING'S SAFETY.

ON SATURDAY, MARCH 25, 1911, A FIRE STARTED ON THE EIGHTH FLOOR OF THE ASCH BUILDING. THIS IS THE STORY OF TWO YOUNG GIRLS CAUGHT IN THAT FIRE. ALTHOUGH THE CHARACTERS ARE FICTIONAL, THE STORY IS BASED ON THE ACTUAL ACCOUNTS OF THOSE WHO SURVIVED THE FIRE.

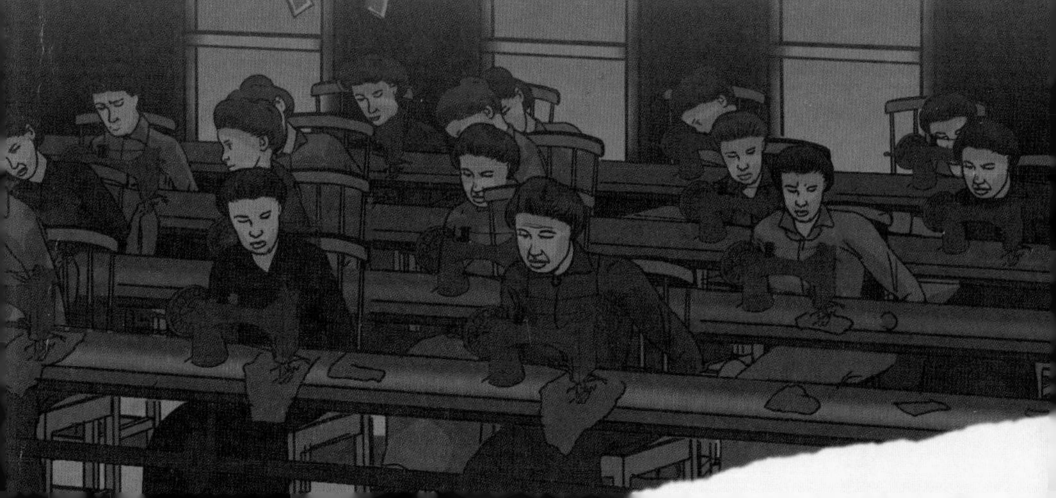

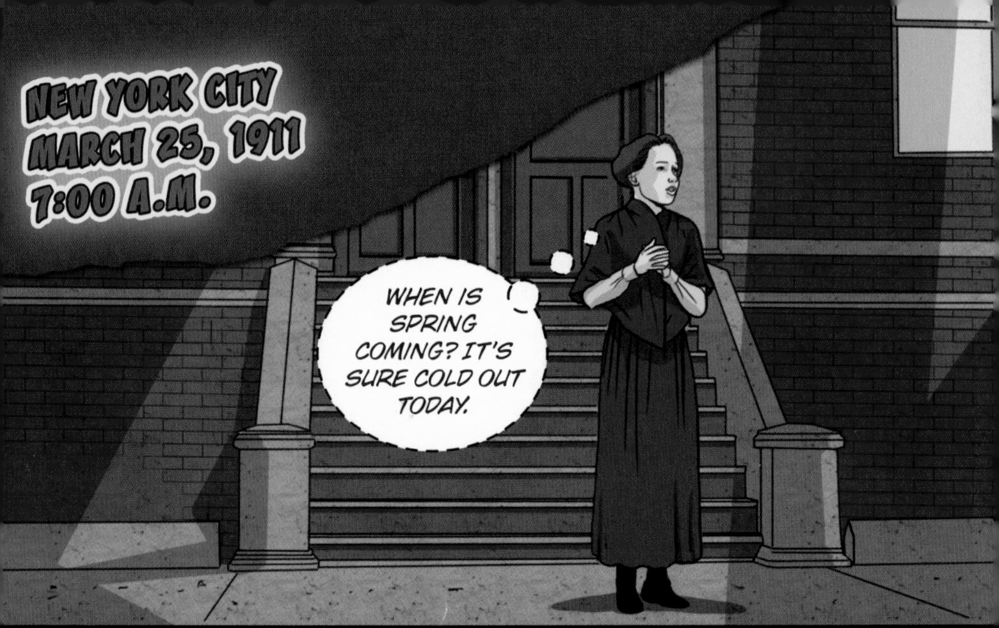
NEW YORK CITY
MARCH 25, 1911
7:00 A.M.
WHEN IS SPRING COMING? IT'S SURE COLD OUT TODAY.

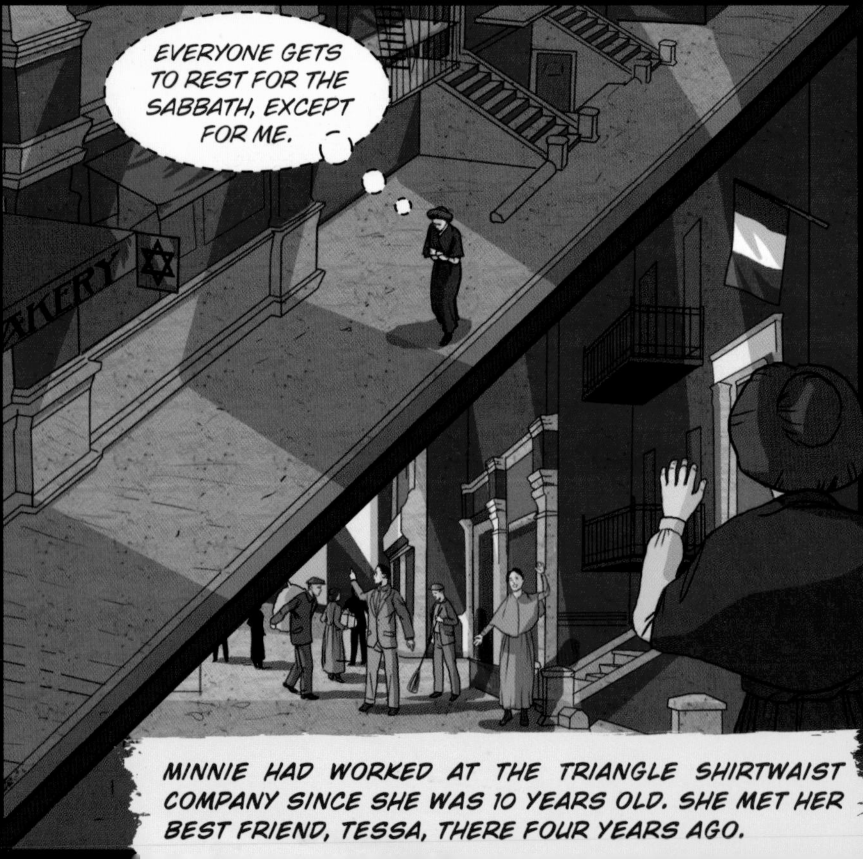
EVERYONE GETS TO REST FOR THE SABBATH, EXCEPT FOR ME.
AKERY
MINNIE HAD WORKED AT THE TRIANGLE SHIRTWAIST COMPANY SINCE SHE WAS 10 YEARS OLD. SHE MET HER BEST FRIEND, TESSA, THERE FOUR YEARS AGO.

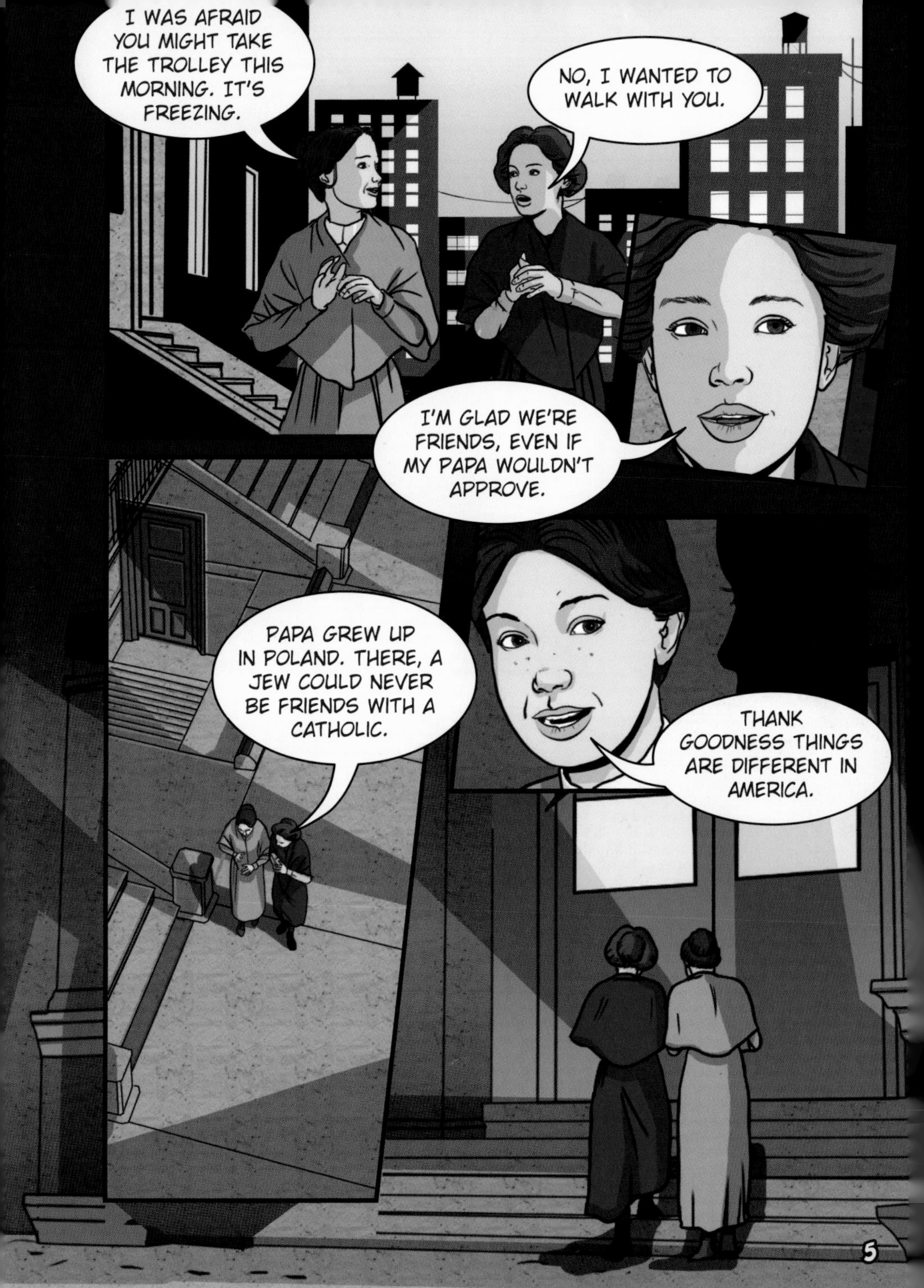
I WAS AFRAID YOU MIGHT TAKE THE TROLLEY THIS MORNING. IT'S FREEZING.
NO, I WANTED TO WALK WITH YOU.
I'M GLAD WE'RE FRIENDS, EVEN IF MY PAPA WOULDN'T APPROVE.
PAPA GREW UP IN POLAND. THERE, A JEW COULD NEVER BE FRIENDS WITH A CATHOLIC.
THANK GOODNESS THINGS ARE DIFFERENT IN AMERICA.

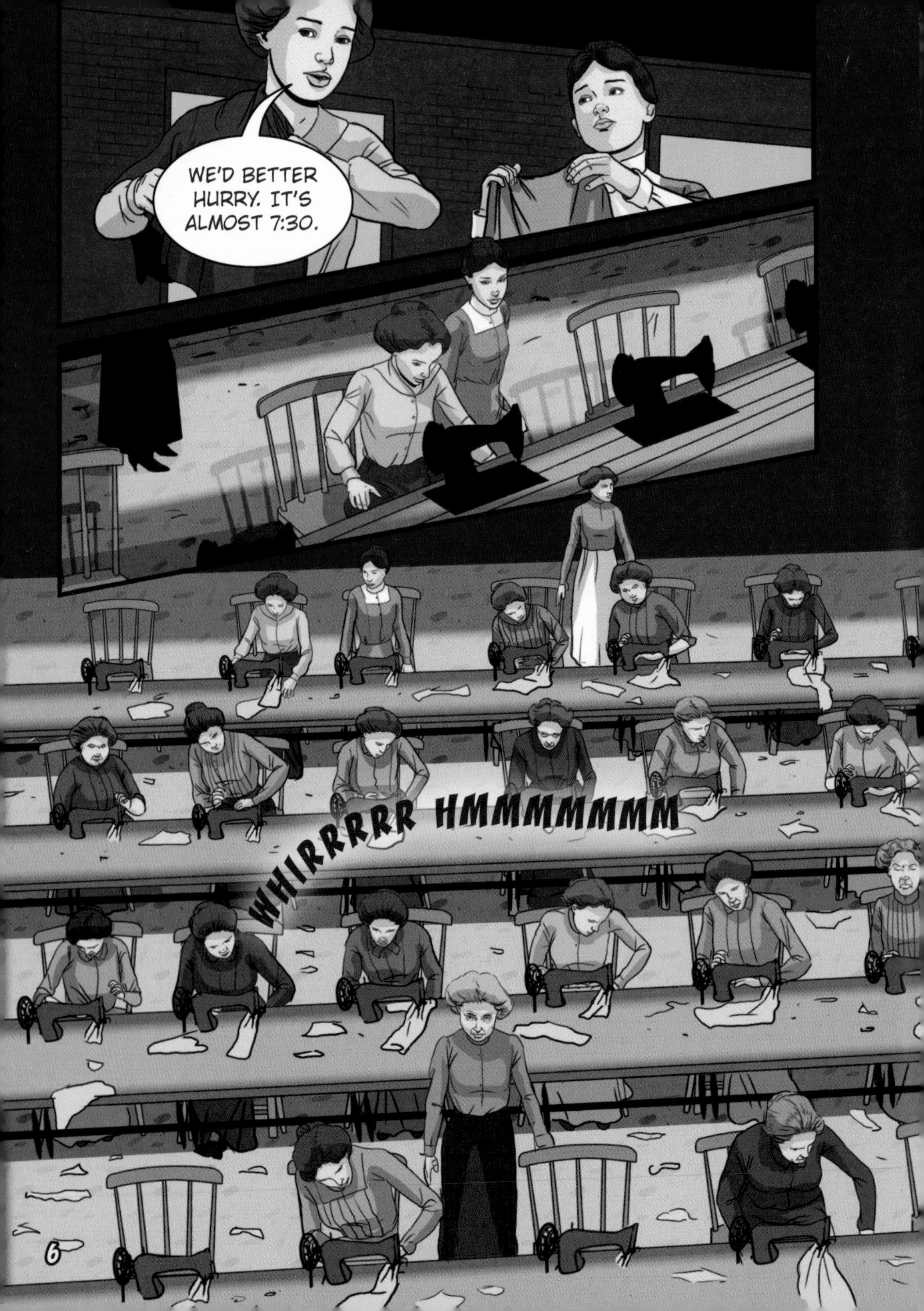
WE'D BETTER HURRY. IT'S ALMOST 7:30.
WHIRRRRR HMMMMMMM

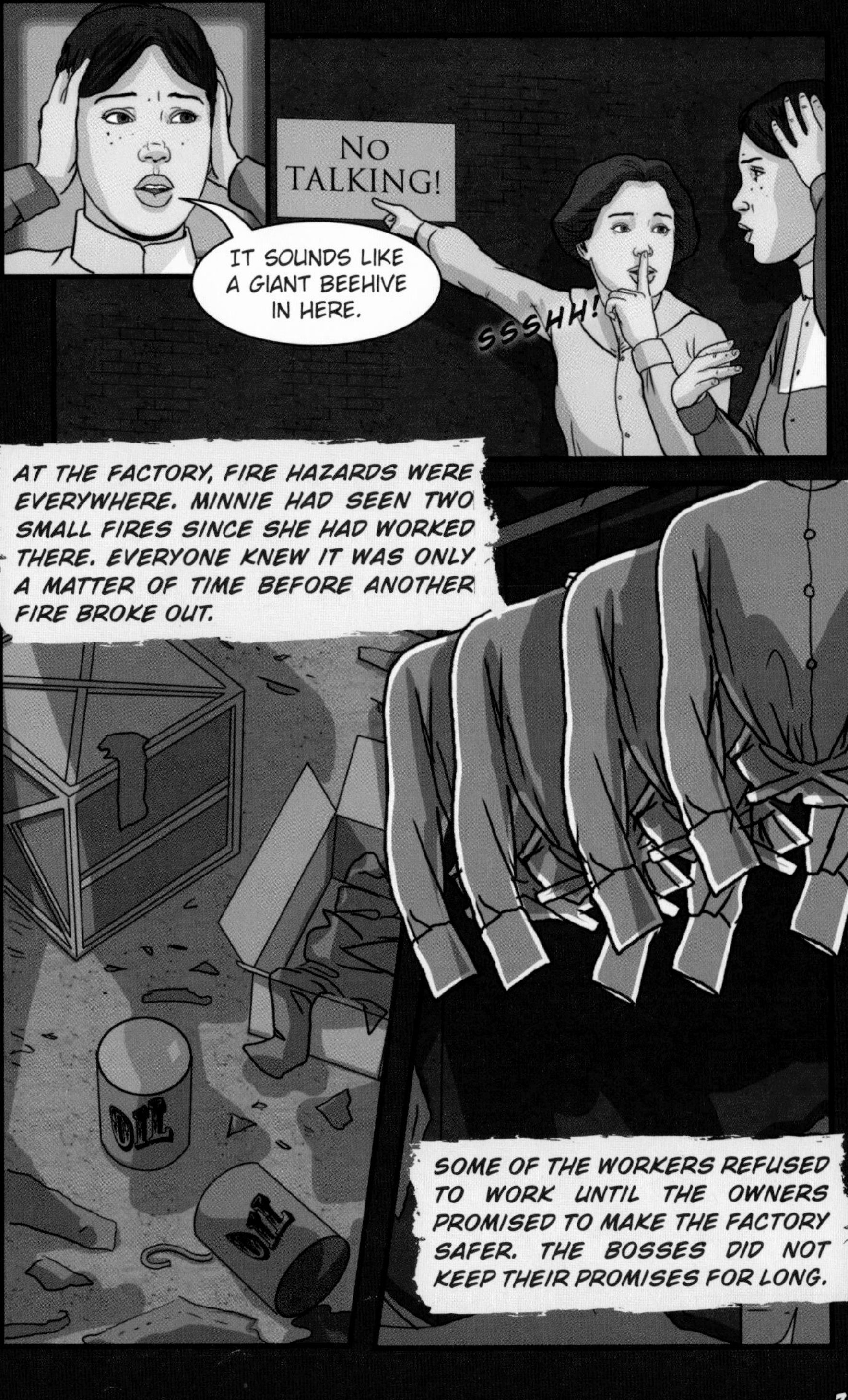
NO TALKING!
IT SOUNDS LIKE A GIANT BEEHIVE IN HERE.
SSSHH!
AT THE FACTORY, FIRE HAZARDS WERE EVERYWHERE. MINNIE HAD SEEN TWO SMALL FIRES SINCE SHE HAD WORKED THERE. EVERYONE KNEW IT WAS ONLY A MATTER OF TIME BEFORE ANOTHER FIRE BROKE OUT.
OIL
OIL
SOME OF THE WORKERS REFUSED TO WORK UNTIL THE OWNERS PROMISED TO MAKE THE FACTORY SAFER. THE BOSSES DID NOT KEEP THEIR PROMISES FOR LONG.

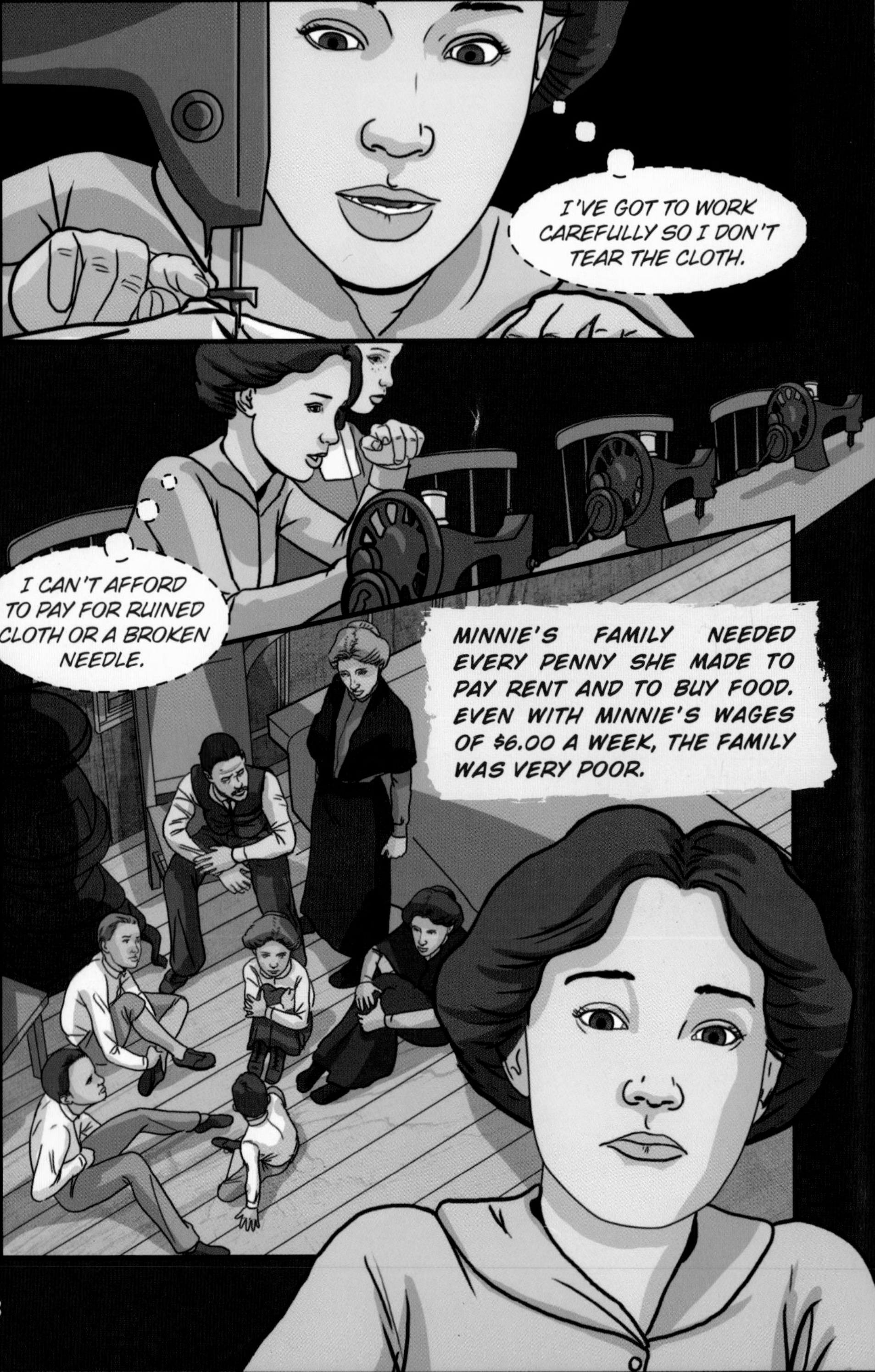
I'VE GOT TO WORK CAREFULLY SO I DON'T TEAR THE CLOTH.
I CAN'T AFFORD TO PAY FOR RUINED CLOTH OR A BROKEN NEEDLE.
MINNIE'S FAMILY NEEDED EVERY PENNY SHE MADE TO PAY RENT AND TO BUY FOOD. EVEN WITH MINNIE'S WAGES OF $6.00 A WEEK, THE FAMILY WAS VERY POOR.

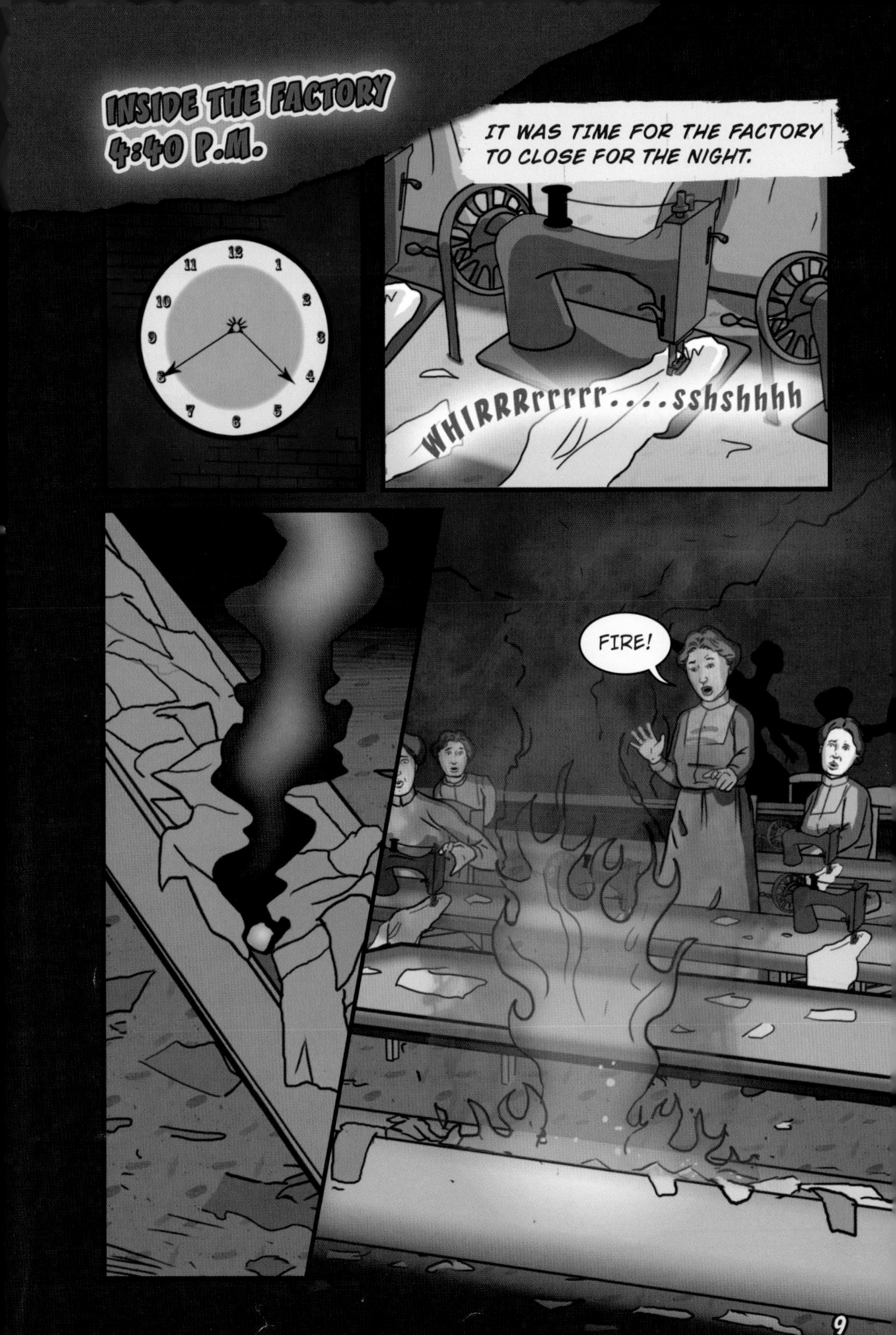

INSIDE THE FACTORY
4:40 P.M.
IT WAS TIME FOR THE FACTORY TO CLOSE FOR THE NIGHT.
WHIRRRrrrrr.....sshshhhh
FIRE!

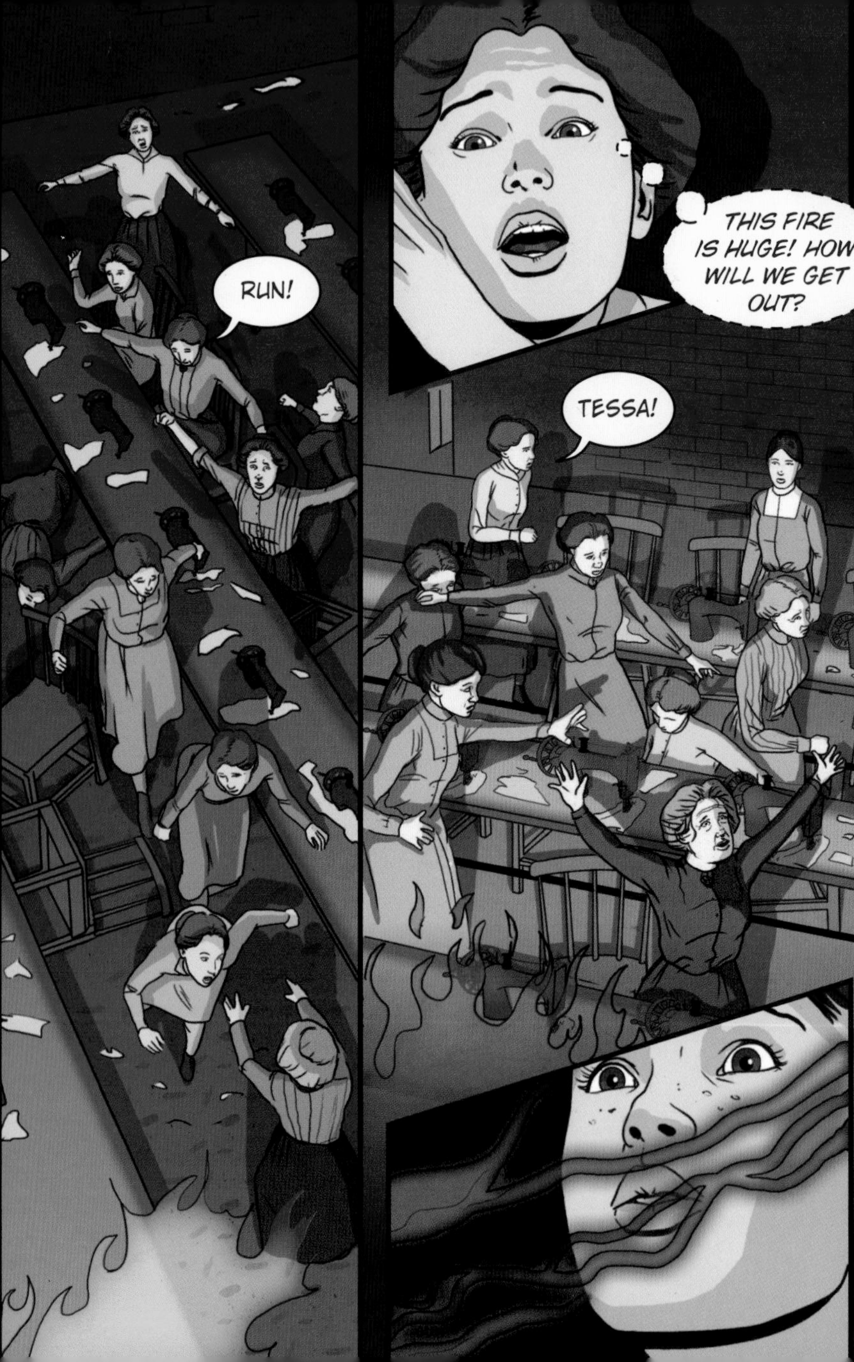
RUN!
THIS FIRE IS HUGE! HOW WILL WE GET OUT?
TESSA!

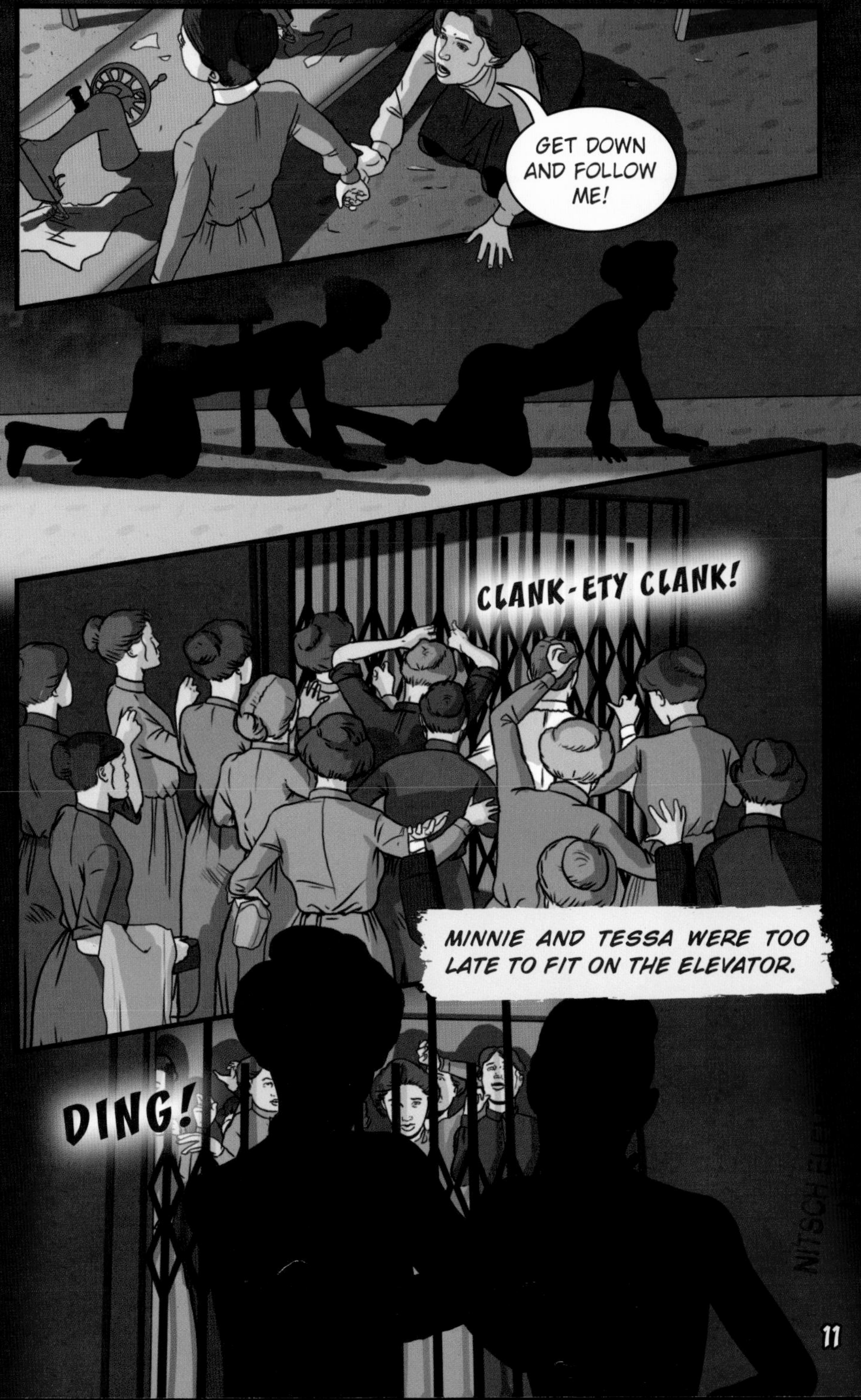
GET DOWN AND FOLLOW ME!
CLANK-ETY CLANK!
MINNIE AND TESSA WERE TOO LATE TO FIT ON THE ELEVATOR.
DING!

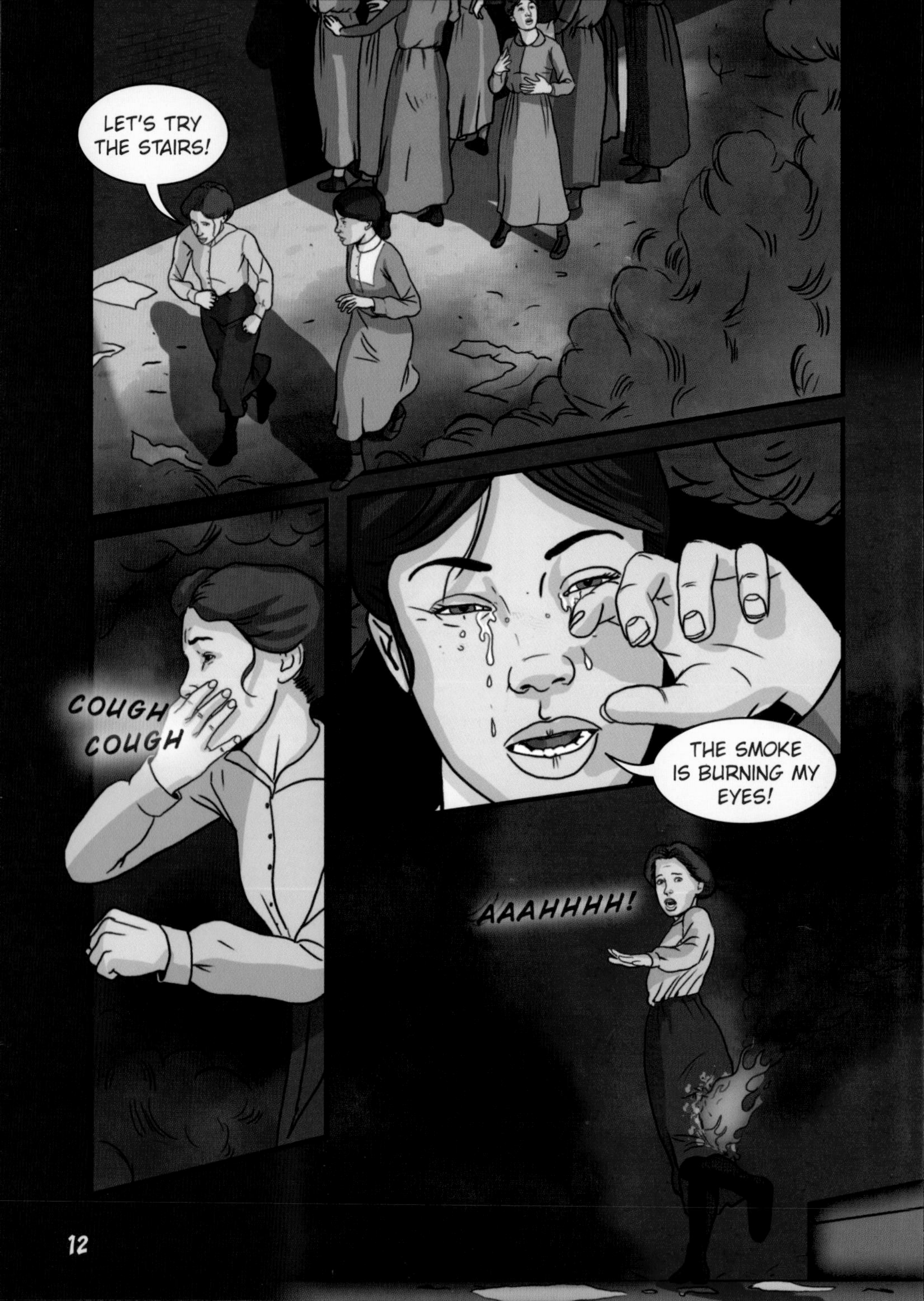
LET'S TRY THE STAIRS!
COUGH COUGH
THE SMOKE IS BURNING MY EYES!
AAAHHHH!

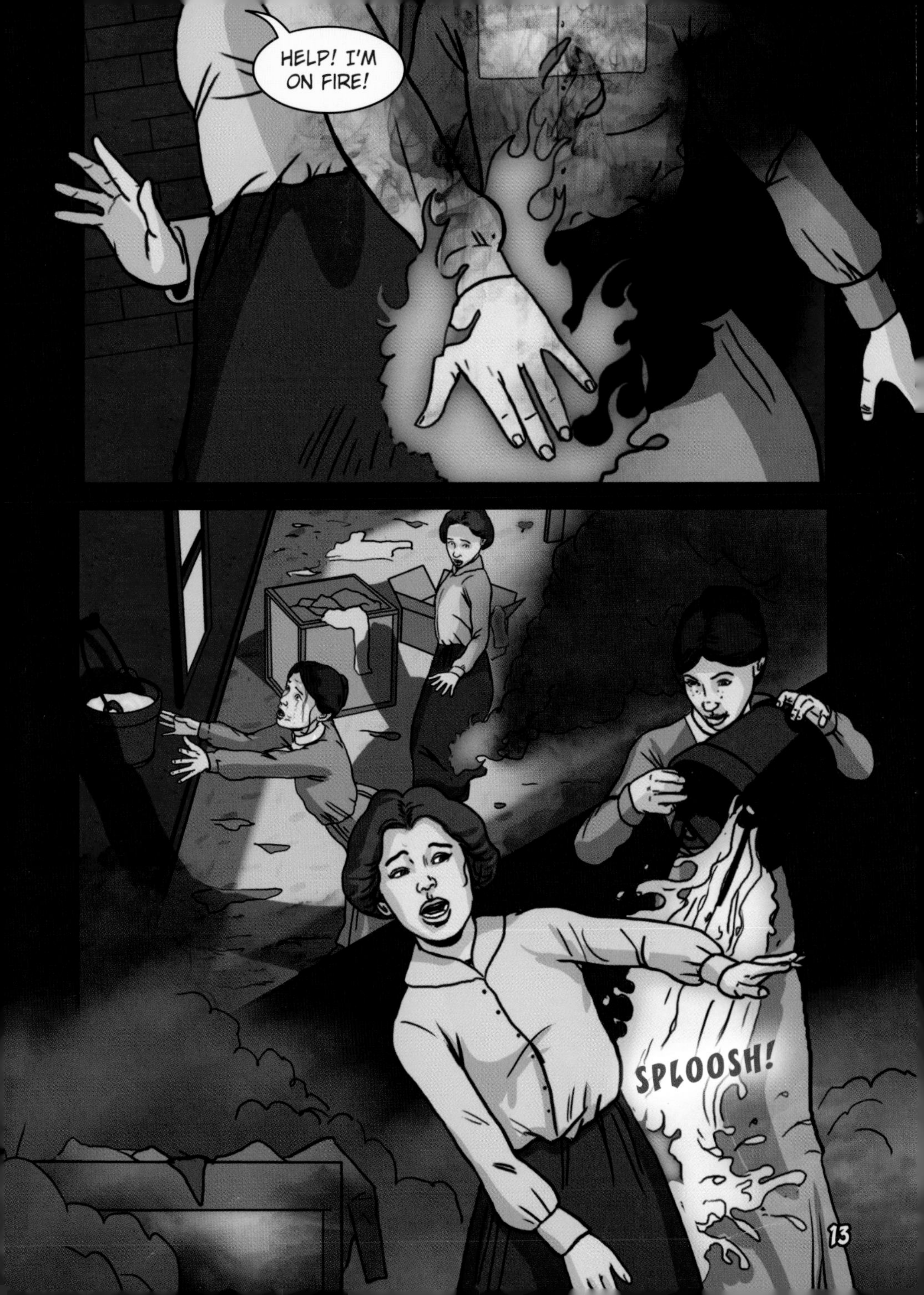
HELP! I'M ON FIRE!
SPLOOSH!

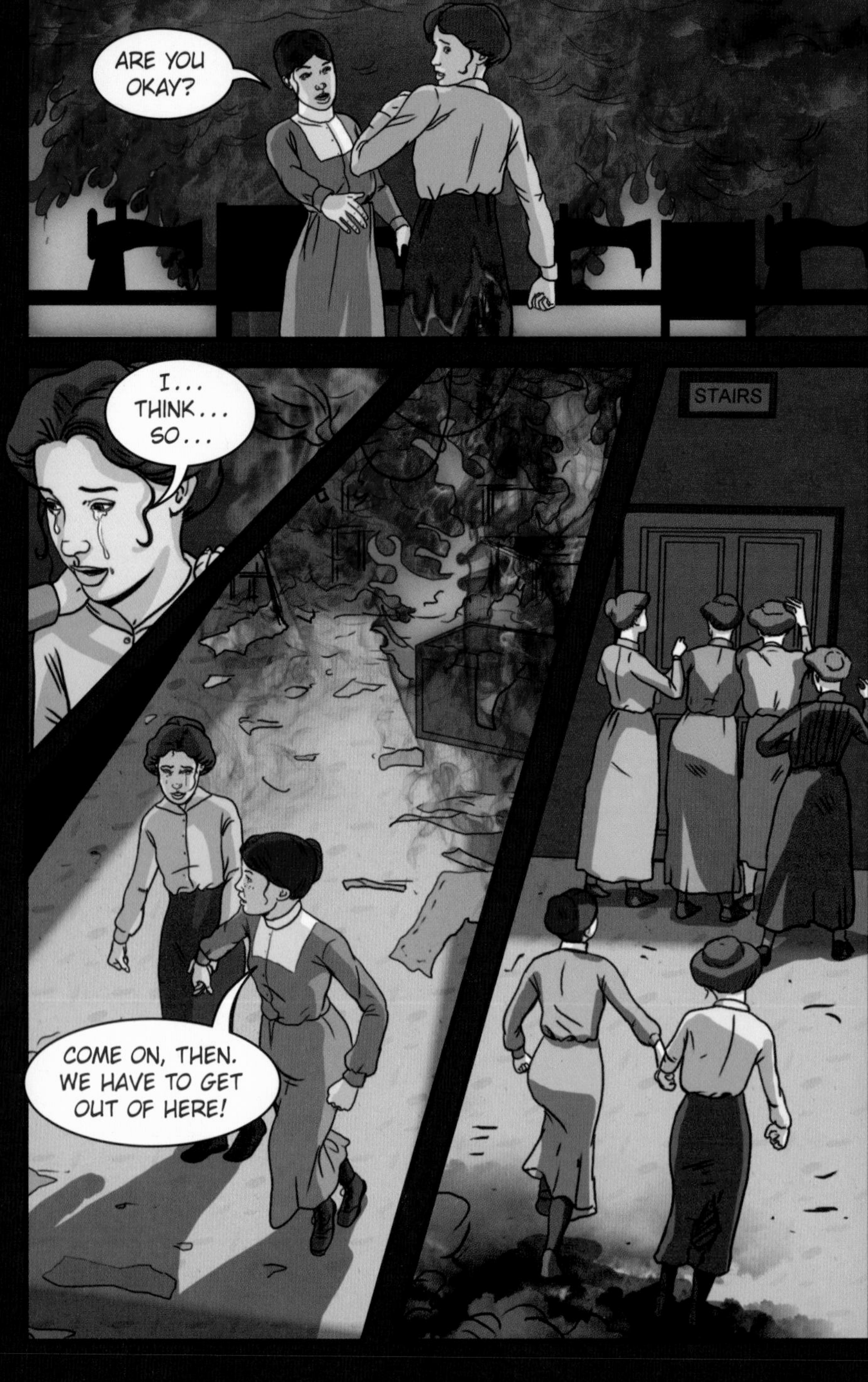
ARE YOU OKAY?
I... THINK... SO...
STAIRS
COME ON, THEN. WE HAVE TO GET OUT OF HERE!

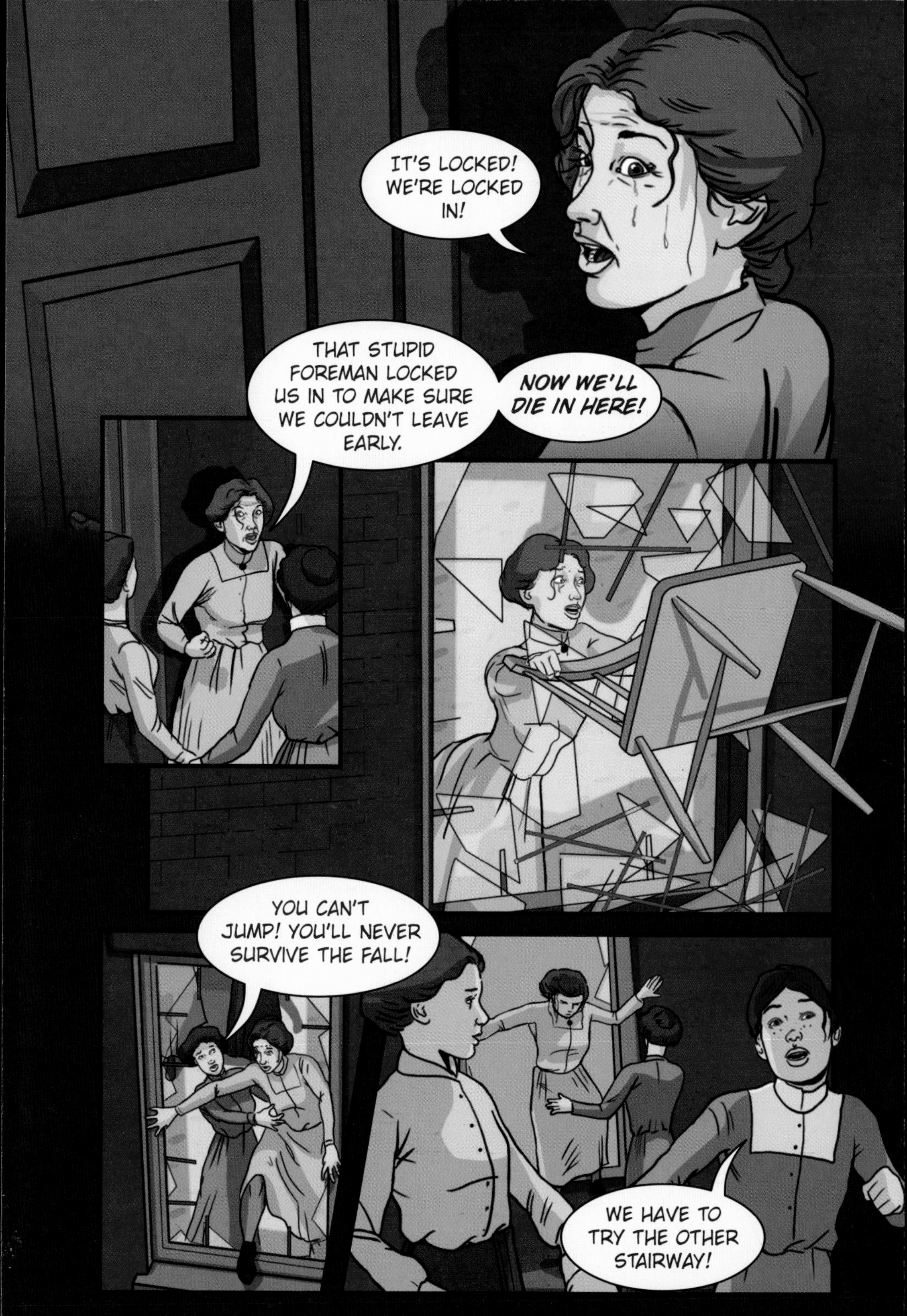
IT'S LOCKED! WE'RE LOCKED IN!
THAT STUPID FOREMAN LOCKED US IN TO MAKE SURE WE COULDN'T LEAVE EARLY.
NOW WE'LL DIE IN HERE!
YOU CAN'T JUMP! YOU'LL NEVER SURVIVE THE FALL!
WE HAVE TO TRY THE OTHER STAIRWAY!

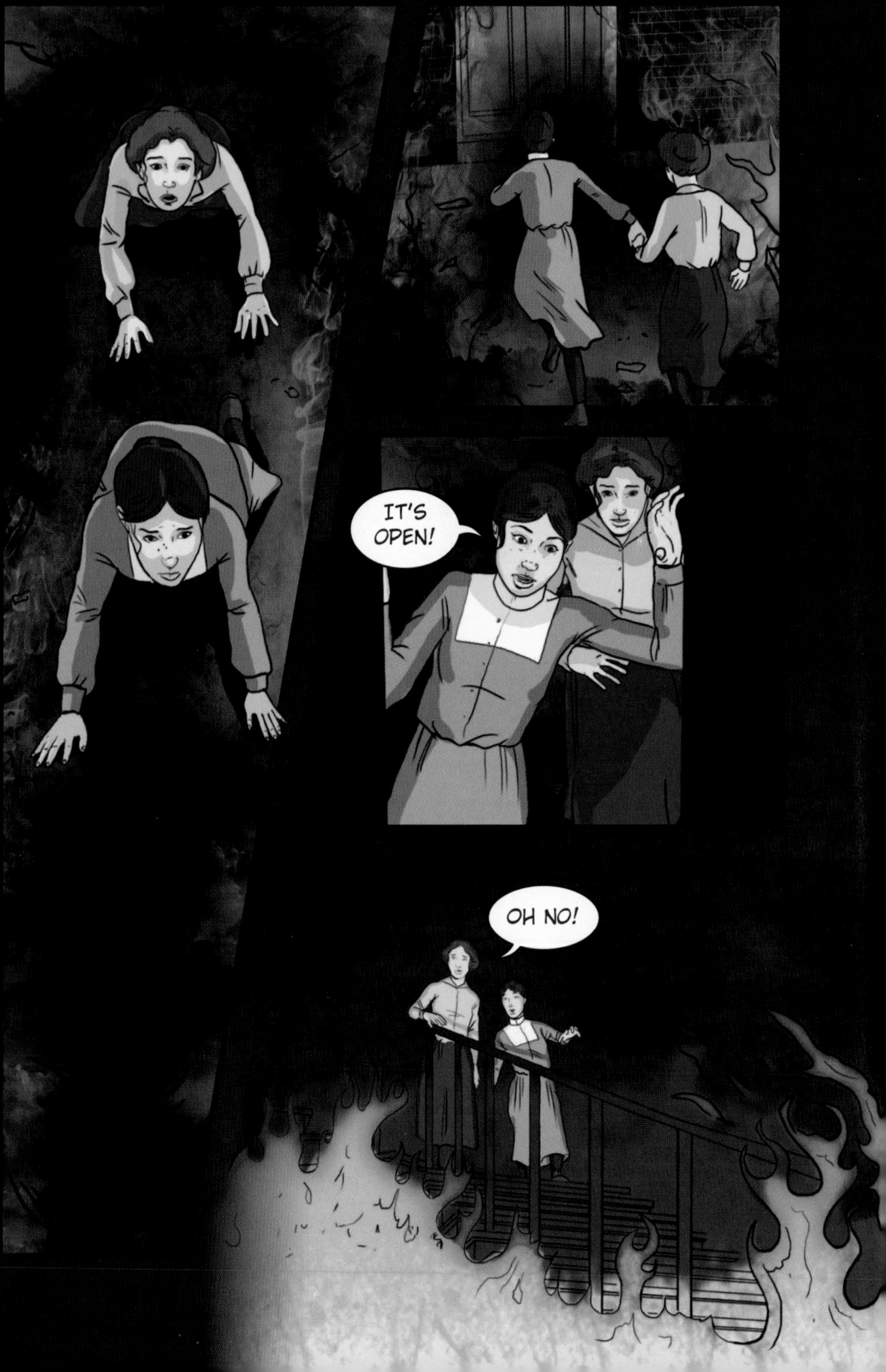
IT'S OPEN!
OH NO!

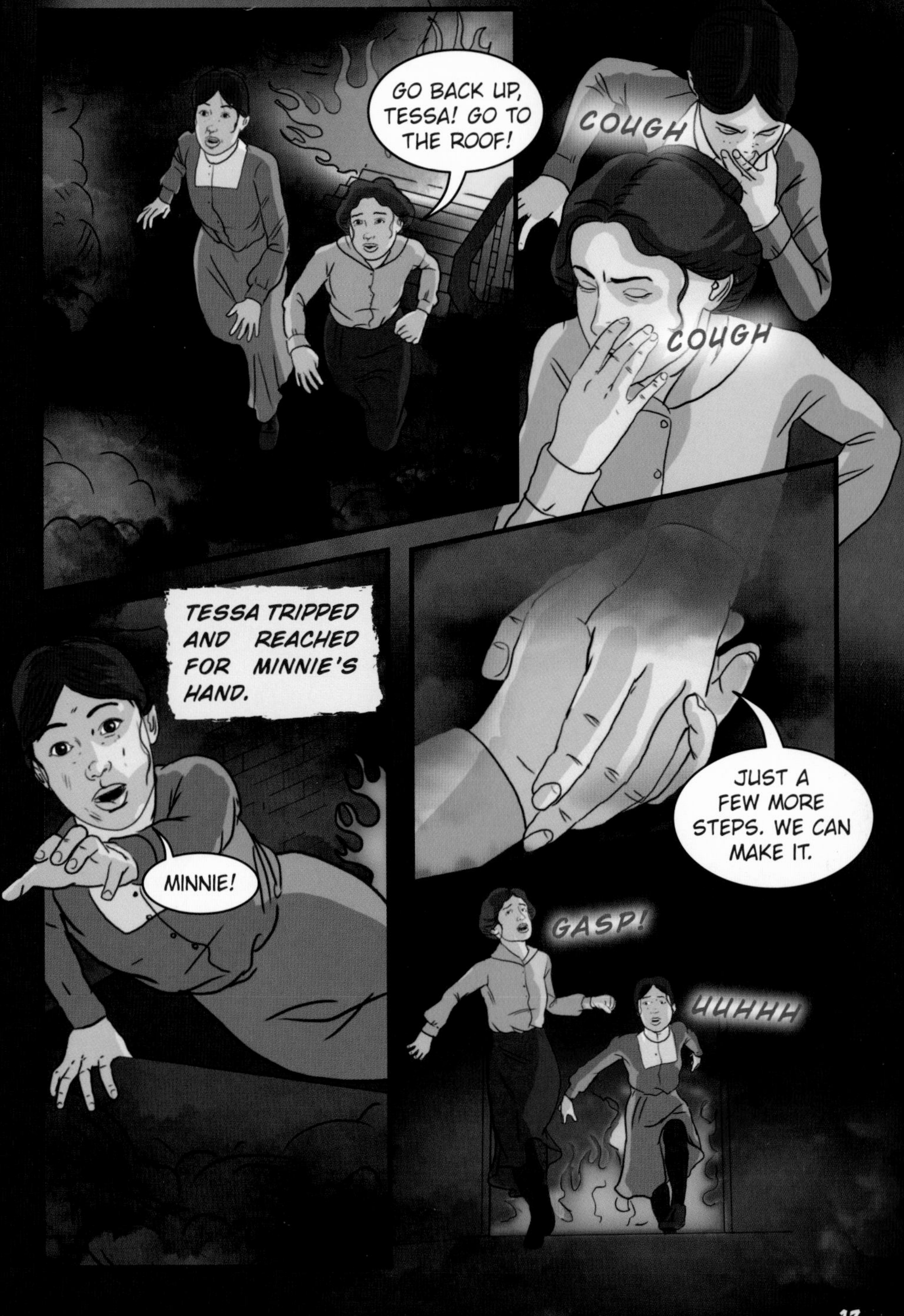
GO BACK UP, TESSA! GO TO THE ROOF!
COUGH
COUGH
TESSA TRIPPED AND REACHED FOR MINNIE'S HAND.
MINNIE!
JUST A FEW MORE STEPS. WE CAN MAKE IT.
GASP!
UUHHH

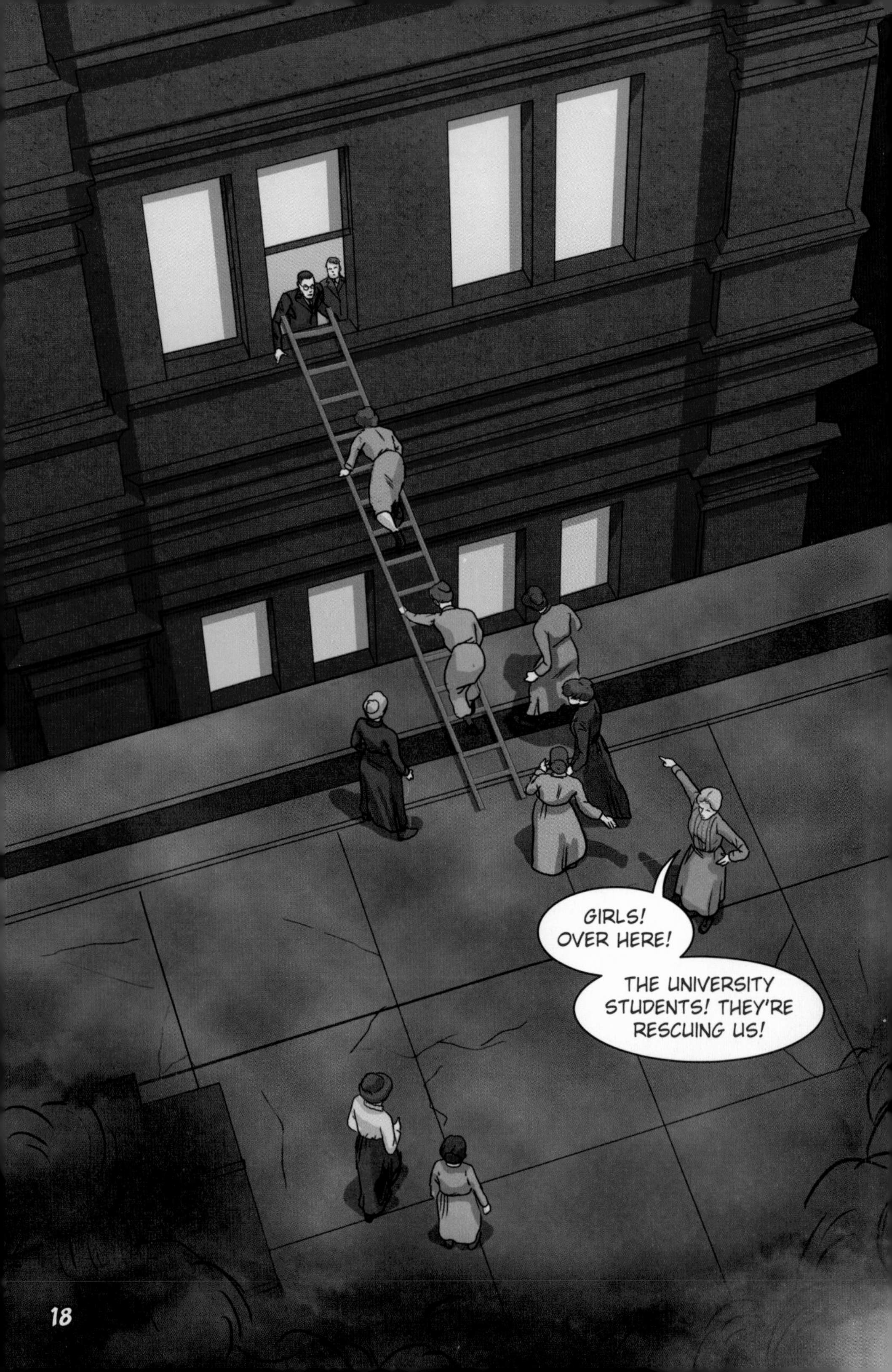
GIRLS! OVER HERE!
THE UNIVERSITY STUDENTS! THEY'RE RESCUING US!

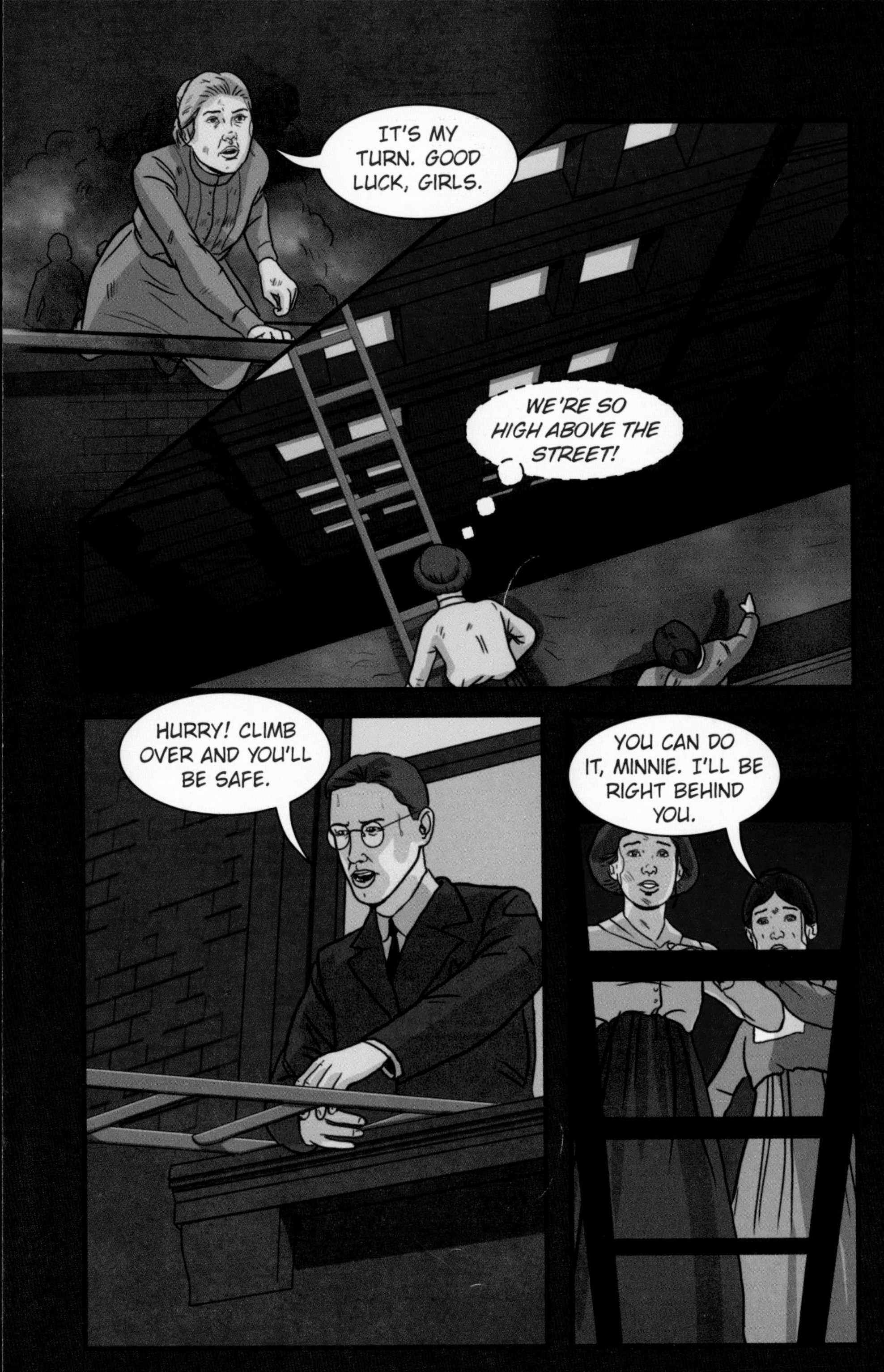

IT'S MY TURN. GOOD LUCK, GIRLS.
WE'RE SO HIGH ABOVE THE STREET!
HURRY! CLIMB OVER AND YOU'LL BE SAFE.
YOU CAN DO IT, MINNIE. I'LL BE RIGHT BEHIND YOU.

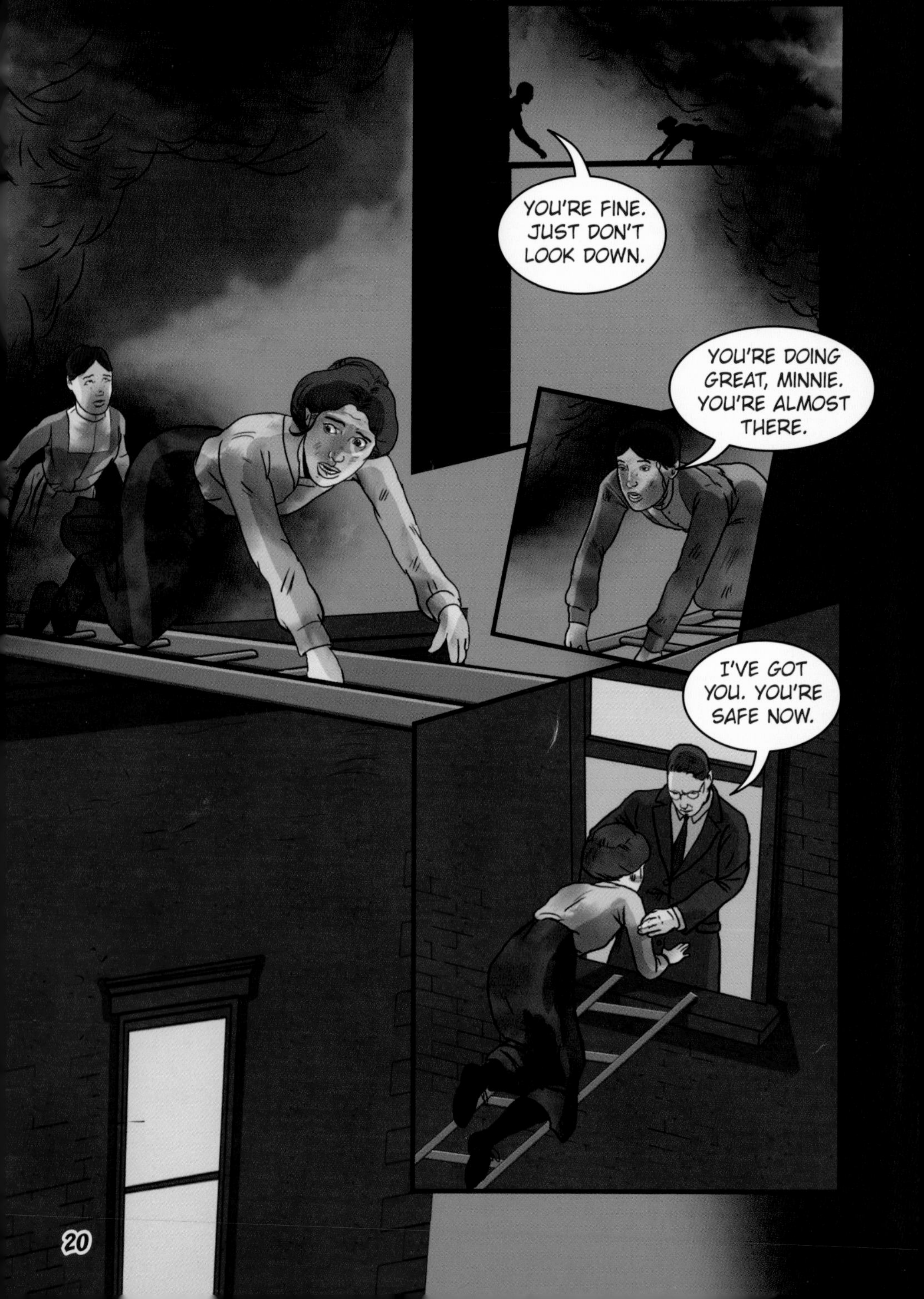
YOU'RE FINE. JUST DON'T LOOK DOWN.
YOU'RE DOING GREAT, MINNIE. YOU'RE ALMOST THERE.
I'VE GOT YOU. YOU'RE SAFE NOW.

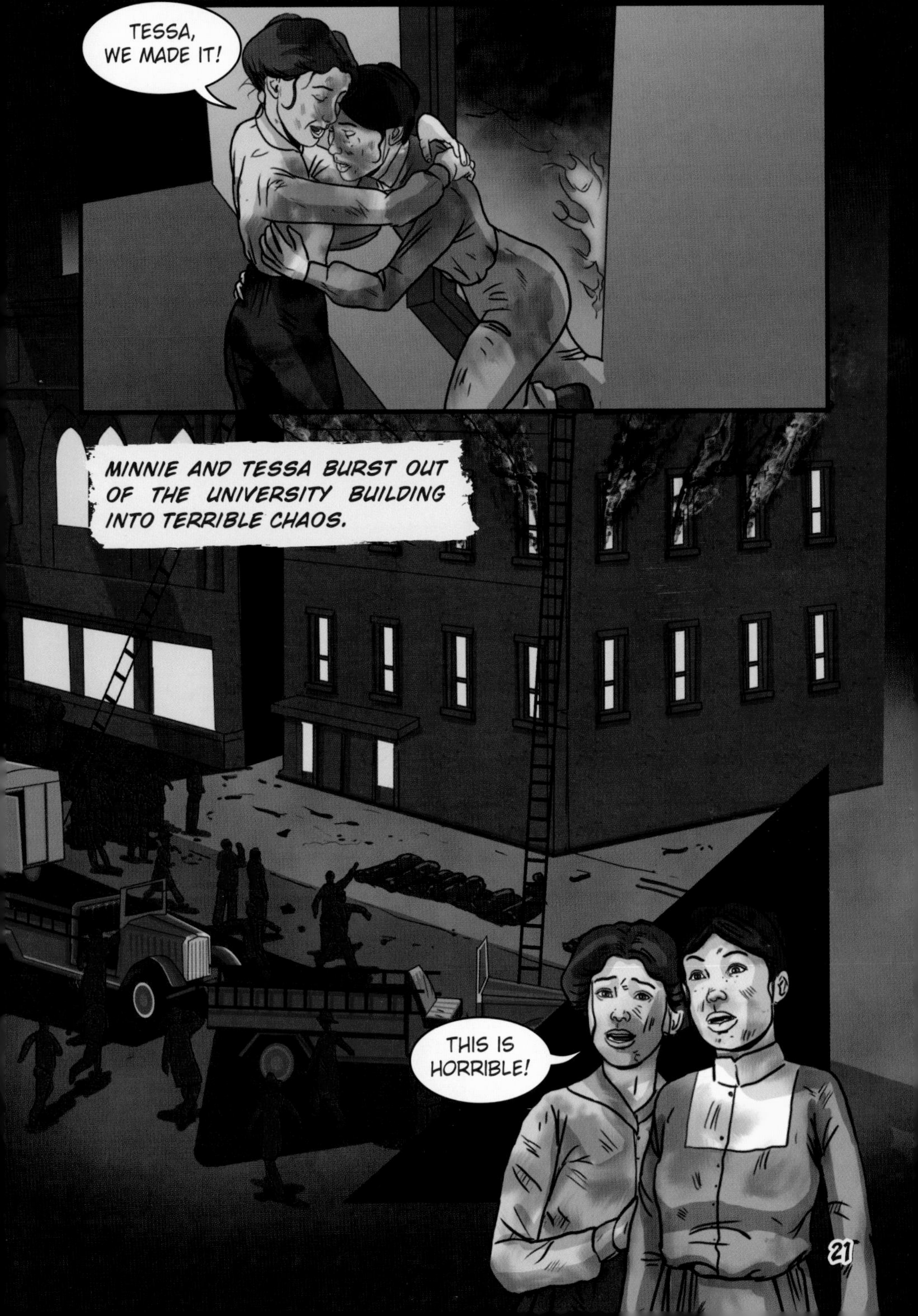

TESSA, WE MADE IT!
MINNIE AND TESSA BURST OUT OF THE UNIVERSITY BUILDING INTO TERRIBLE CHAOS.
THIS IS HORRIBLE!

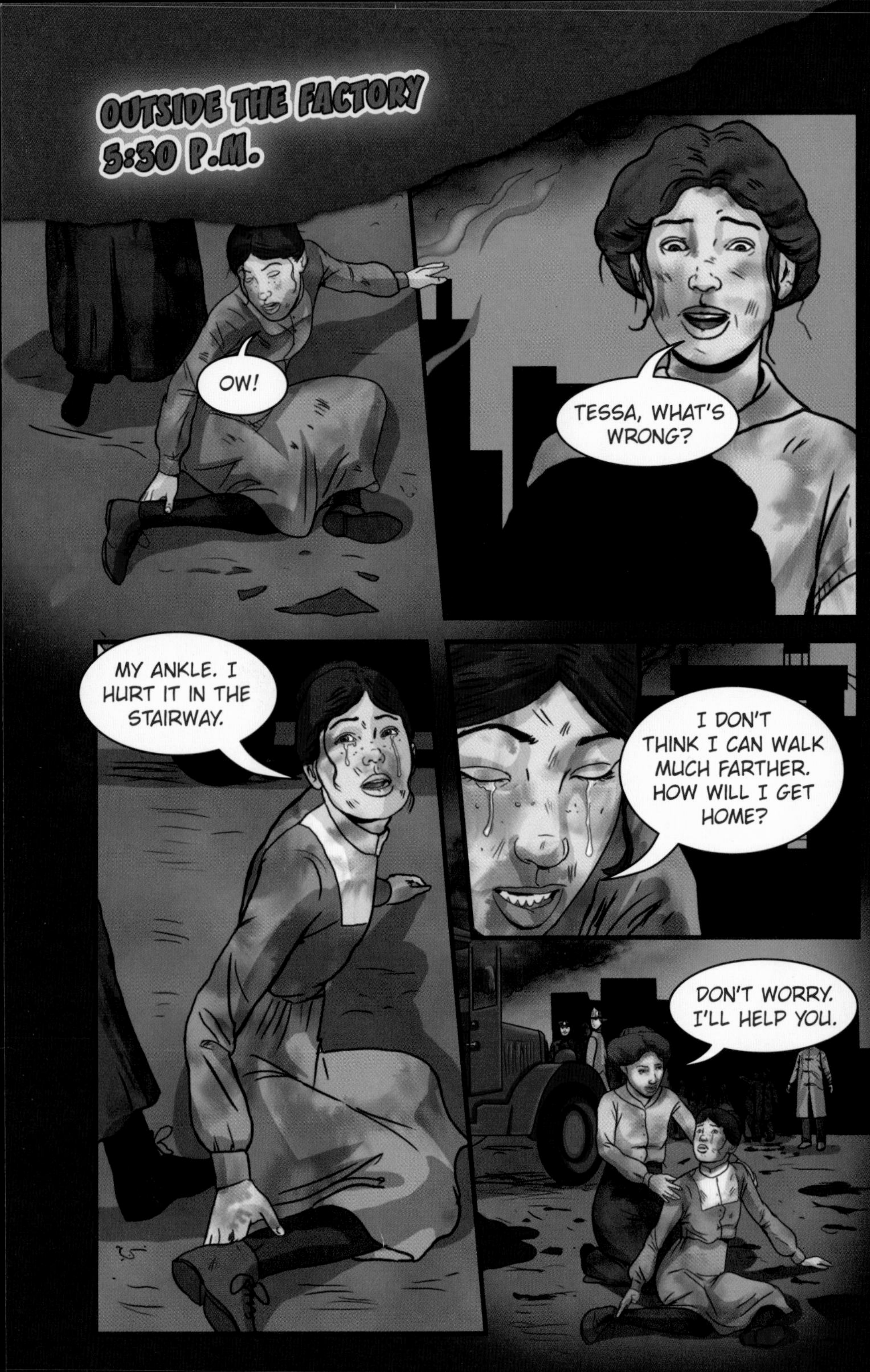
OUTSIDE THE FACTORY
5:30 P.M.
OW!
TESSA, WHAT'S WRONG?
MY ANKLE. I HURT IT IN THE STAIRWAY.
I DON'T THINK I CAN WALK MUCH FARTHER. HOW WILL I GET HOME?
DON'T WORRY. I'LL HELP YOU.

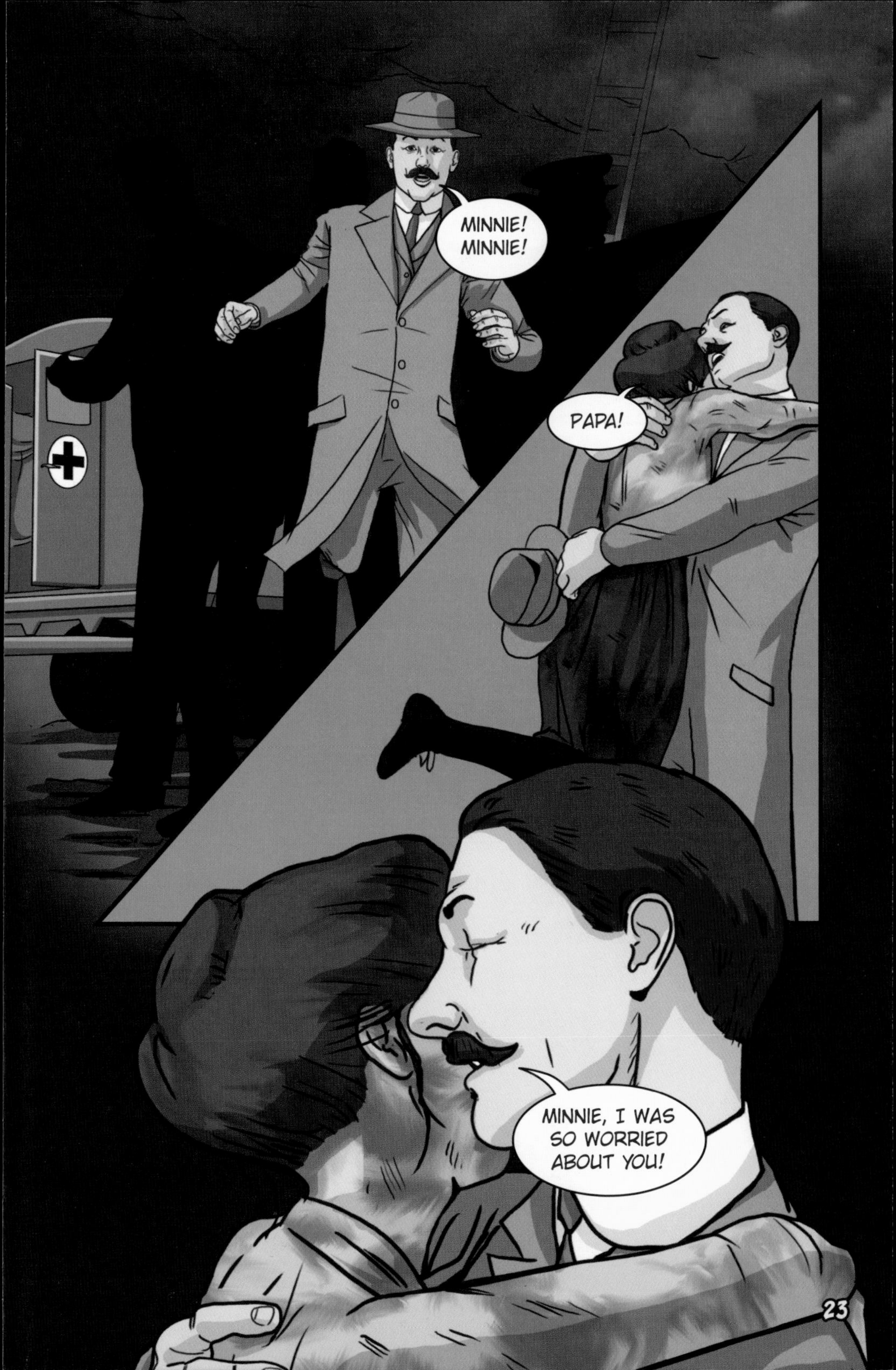
MINNIE!
MINNIE!
PAPA!
MINNIE, I WAS SO WORRIED ABOUT YOU!

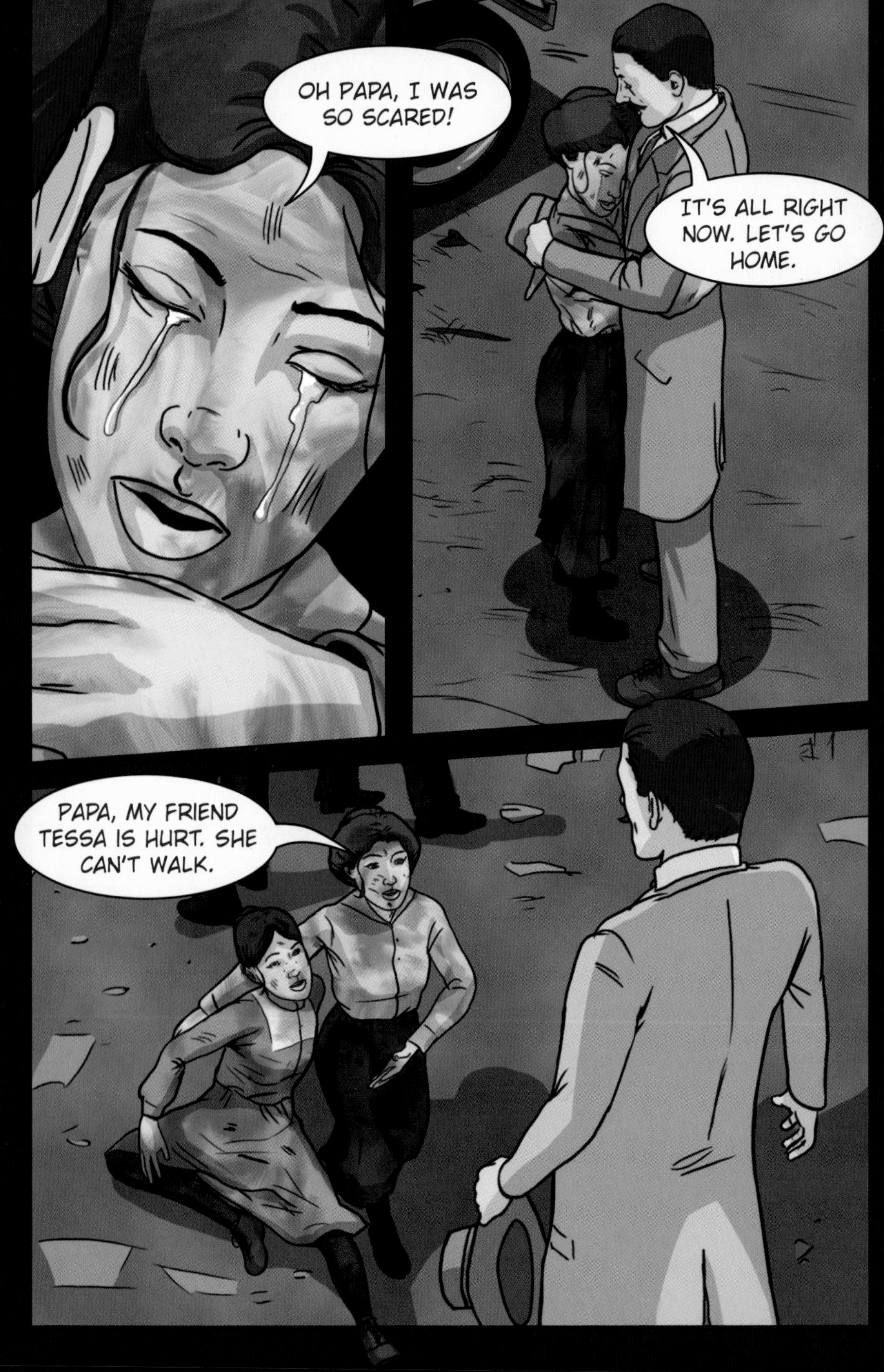
OH PAPA, I WAS SO SCARED!
IT'S ALL RIGHT NOW. LET'S GO HOME.
PAPA, MY FRIEND TESSA IS HURT. SHE CAN'T WALK.

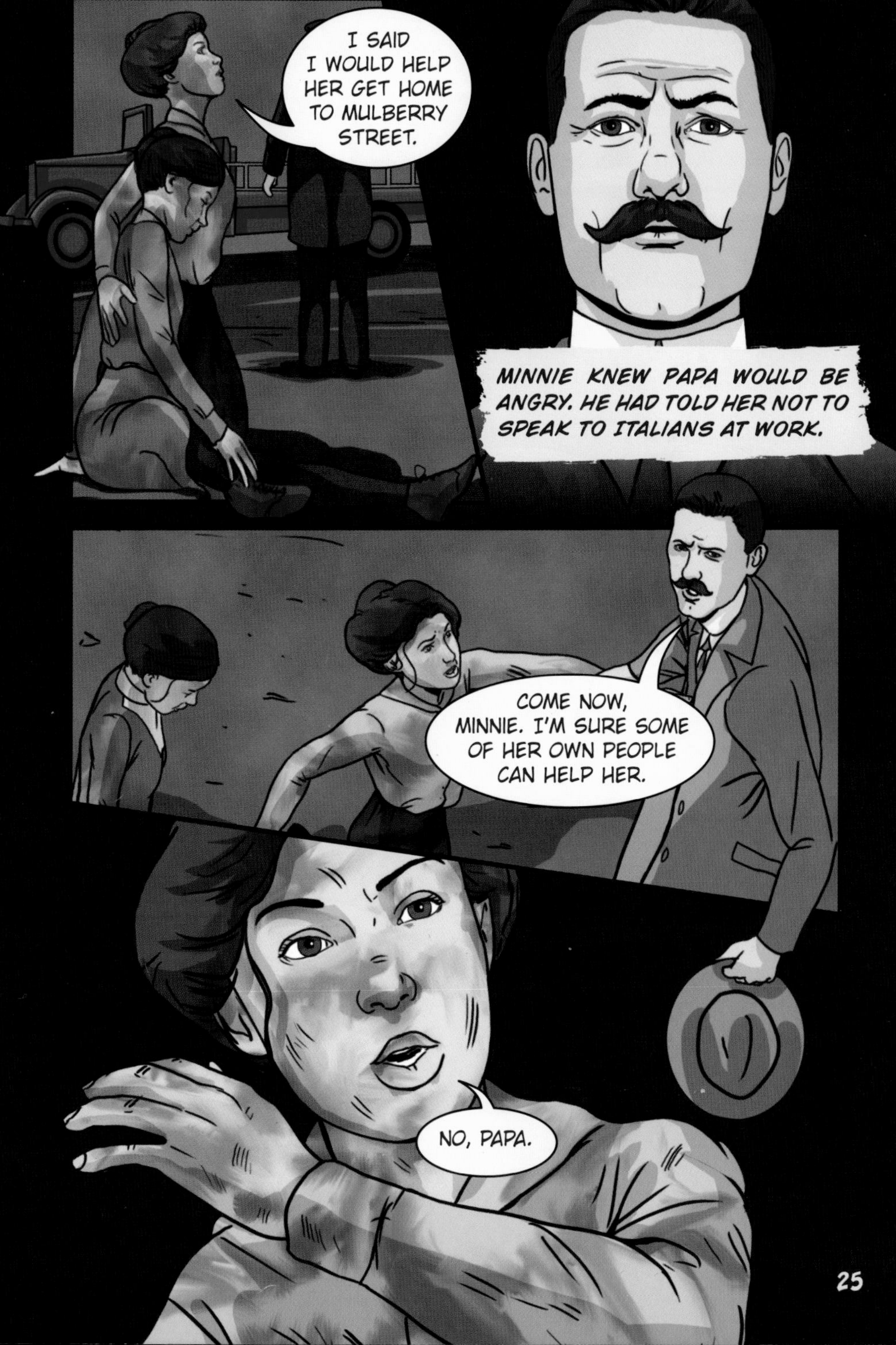
I SAID I WOULD HELP HER GET HOME TO MULBERRY STREET.
MINNIE KNEW PAPA WOULD BE ANGRY. HE HAD TOLD HER NOT TO SPEAK TO ITALIANS AT WORK.
COME NOW, MINNIE. I'M SURE SOME OF HER OWN PEOPLE CAN HELP HER.
NO, PAPA.

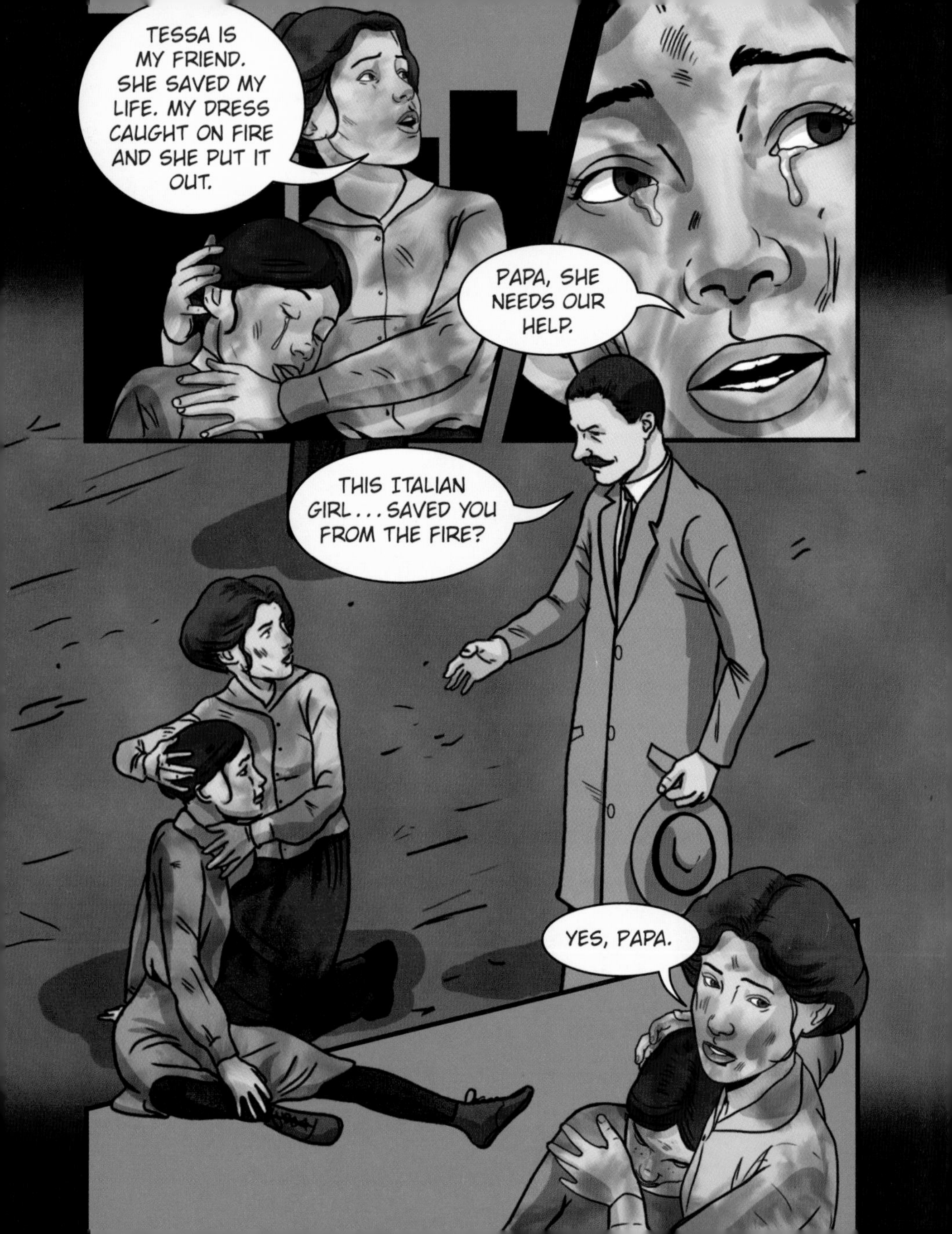
TESSA IS MY FRIEND. SHE SAVED MY LIFE. MY DRESS CAUGHT ON FIRE AND SHE PUT IT OUT.
PAPA, SHE NEEDS OUR HELP.
THIS ITALIAN GIRL . . . SAVED YOU FROM THE FIRE?
YES, PAPA.

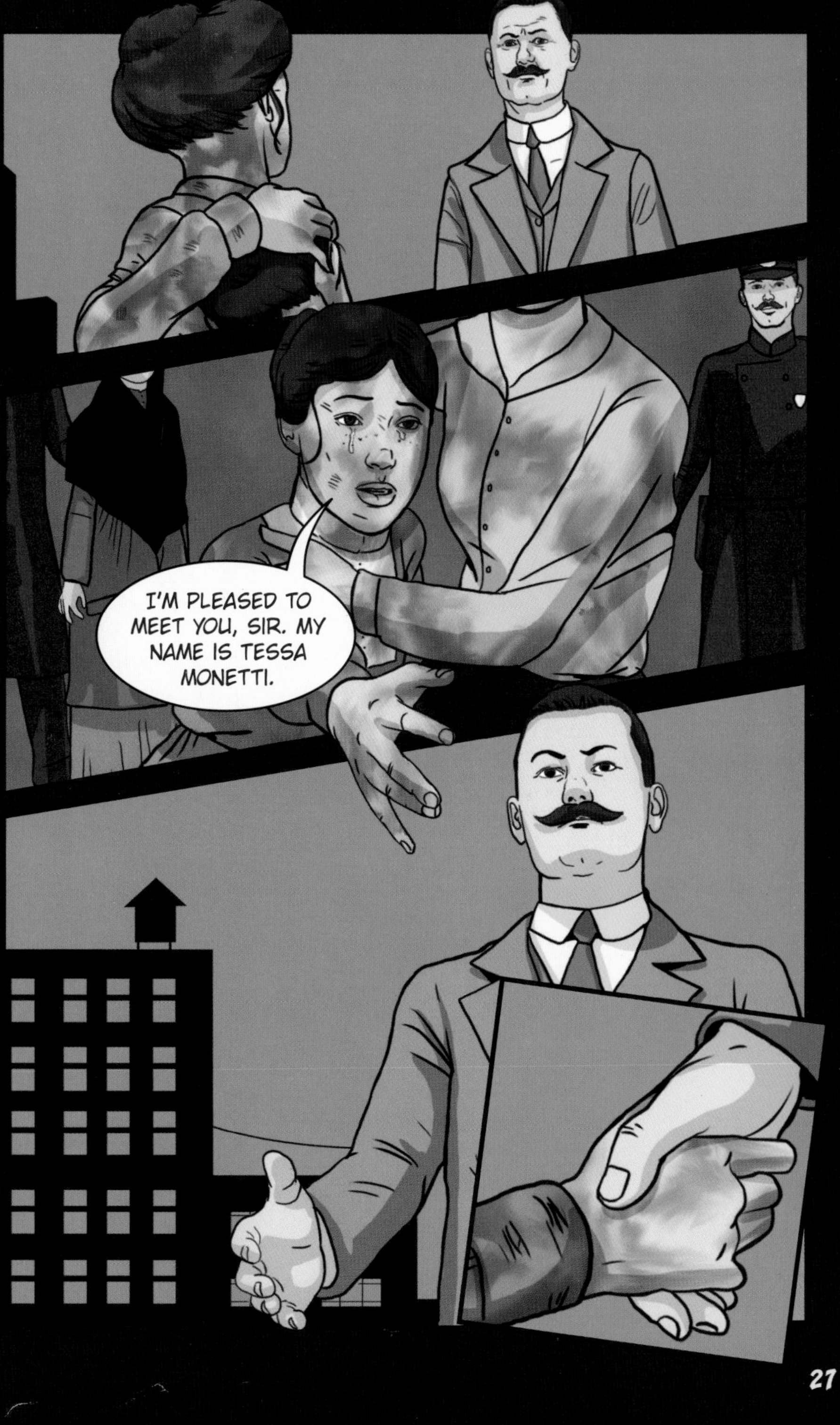
I'M PLEASED TO MEET YOU, SIR. MY NAME IS TESSA MONETTI.

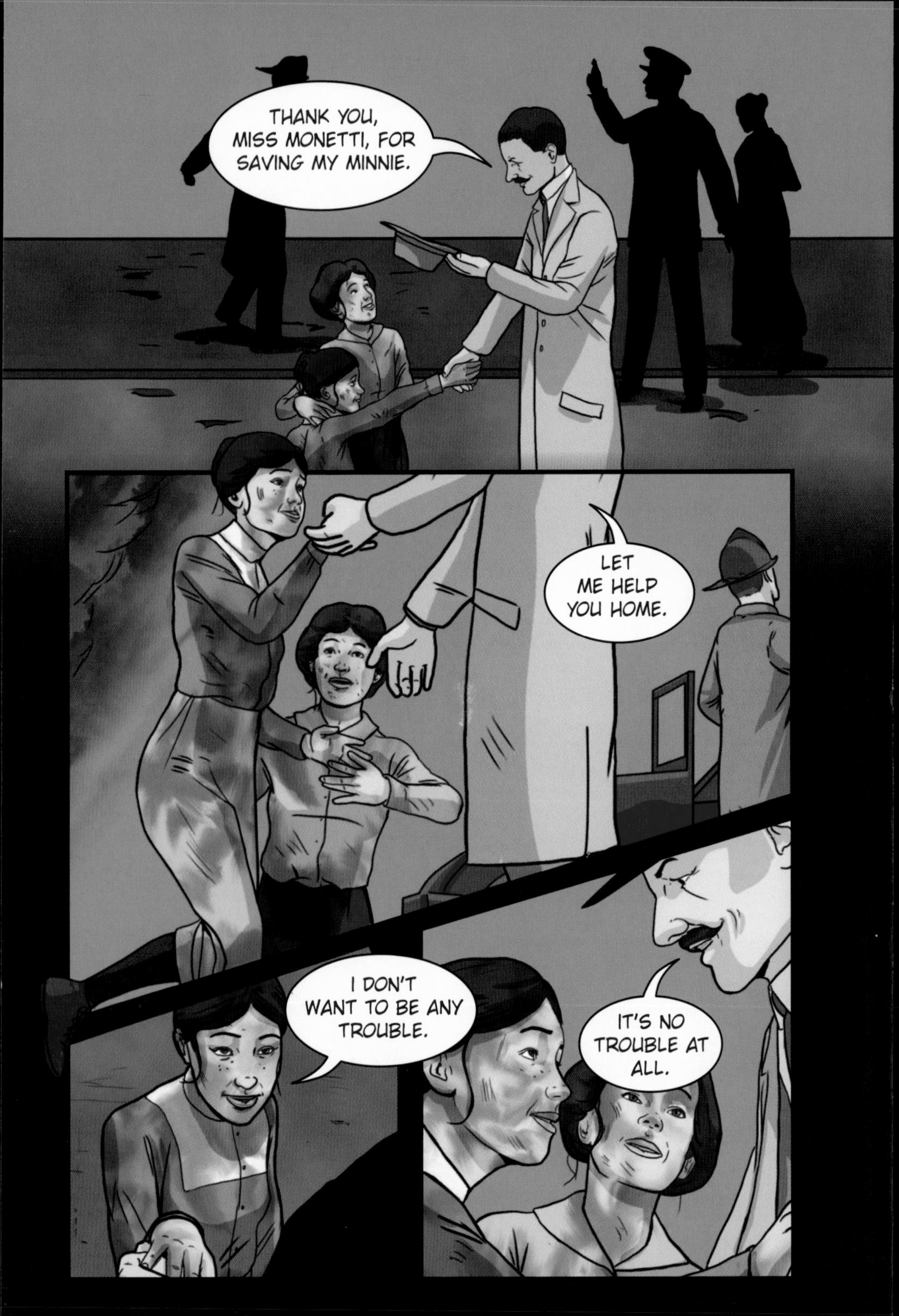
THANK YOU, MISS MONETTI, FOR SAVING MY MINNIE.
LET ME HELP YOU HOME.
I DON'T WANT TO BE ANY TROUBLE.
IT'S NO TROUBLE AT ALL.

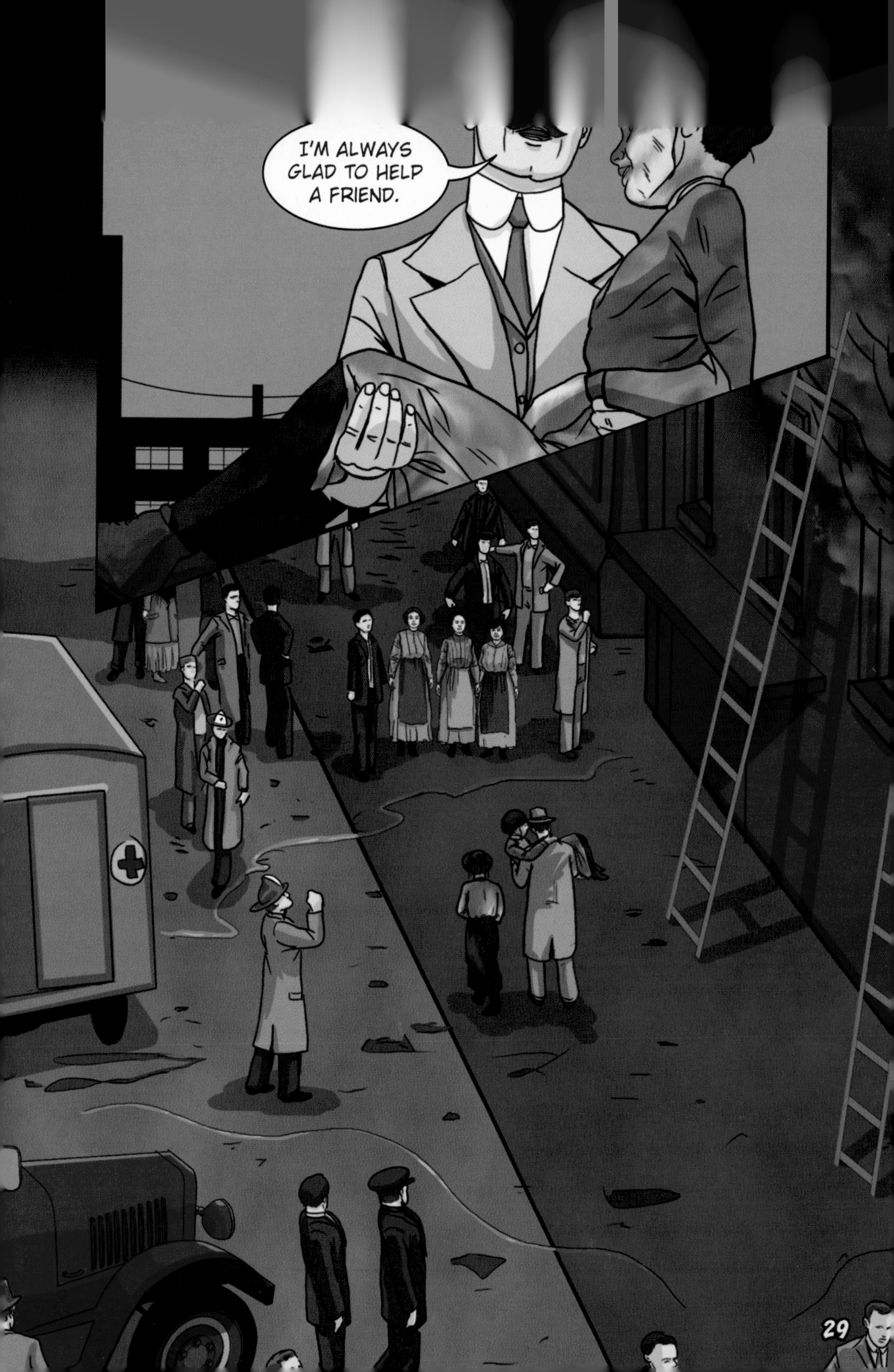
I'M ALWAYS GLAD TO HELP A FRIEND.

AFTERWORD

IN LESS THAN HALF AN HOUR, 146 OF THE FACTORY WORKERS WERE DEAD. AFTERWARD, PEOPLE WERE ANGRY THAT A FIRE LIKE THIS COULD HAVE HAPPENED. WHY WEREN'T THERE MORE FIRE ESCAPES? WHY WERE THE DOORS LOCKED? IN THE TRIAL THAT FOLLOWED, THE FACTORY OWNERS WERE FOUND INNOCENT OF ANY WRONGDOING. THE TRIANGLE FACTORY HAD MET ALL THE SAFETY CONDITIONS REQUIRED BY LAW.

MANY PEOPLE FELT THE LAWS NEEDED TO BE CHANGED. MODERN FACTORIES MUST HAVE FIRE ALARMS, MULTIPLE EXITS, AND FIRE ESCAPES. FACTORIES NEED A SPRINKLER SYSTEM THAT WILL AUTOMATICALLY SHOWER WATER ON A FIRE. THEY ARE ALSO REQUIRED TO HOLD FIRE DRILLS SO THAT WORKERS WILL KNOW HOW TO ESCAPE IF A FIRE BREAKS OUT. IT MIGHT NOT BE POSSIBLE TO PREVENT FACTORY FIRES COMPLETELY, BUT PERHAPS BECAUSE OF THE FIRE AT THE TRIANGLE FACTORY, NEVER AGAIN WILL SO MANY PEOPLE HAVE TO DIE IN ONE.

FURTHER READING AND WEBSITES

BRILL, MARLENE TARG. *ANNIE SHAPIRO AND THE CLOTHING WORKERS' STRIKE*. MINNEAPOLIS: MILLBROOK PRESS, 2011.

CEFREY, HOLLY. *INDUSTRIAL GROWTH IN NEW YORK*. NEW YORK: ROSEN, 2003.

GREENE, JACQUELINE DEMBAR. *THE TRIANGLE SHIRTWAIST FACTORY FIRE*. NEW YORK: BEARPORT PUBLISHING, 2007.

LEVINE, ELLEN. *IF YOUR NAME WAS CHANGED AT ELLIS ISLAND*. NEW YORK: SCHOLASTIC, 2006.

NELSON, ROBIN. *FROM COTTON TO T-SHIRT*. MINNEAPOLIS: LERNER PUBLICATIONS COMPANY, 2003.

NEWMAN, PAULINE, AND JOAN MORRISON. "WORKING FOR THE TRIANGLE SHIRTWAIST COMPANY."
HTTP://HISTORYMATTERS.GMU.EDU/D/178/

PBS KIDS *GO!* BIG APPLE HISTORY: NEW YORK LIVING
HTTP://PBSKIDS.ORG/BIGAPPLEHISTORY/LIFE/INDEX-FLASH.HTML

PLATT, RICHARD. *THROUGH TIME: NEW YORK CITY*. NEW YORK: KINGFISHER, 2010.

PRICE, SEAN. *SMOKESTACKS AND SPINNING JENNYS: INDUSTRIAL REVOLUTION*. CHICAGO: RAINTREE, 2007.

ABOUT THE AUTHOR

HOLLY LITTLEFIELD HAS PUBLISHED SEVERAL CHILDREN'S BOOKS ON TOPICS RANGING FROM JAPAN TO AMERICAN PIONEER CHILDREN. SHE LIVES IN MAPLE GROVE, MINNESOTA.

ABOUT THE ADAPTER

AMANDA DOERING TOURVILLE HAS WRITTEN MORE THAN 40 BOOKS FOR CHILDREN. TOURVILLE IS GREATLY HONORED TO WRITE FOR YOUNG PEOPLE AND HOPES THAT THEY WILL LEARN TO LOVE READING AND LEARNING AS MUCH AS SHE DOES. WHEN NOT WRITING, TOURVILLE ENJOYS TRAVELING, PHOTOGRAPHY, AND HIKING. SHE LIVES IN MINNESOTA WITH HER HUSBAND AND GUINEA PIG.

ABOUT THE ILLUSTRATORS

TED HAMMOND IS A CANADIAN ARTIST, LIVING AND WORKING JUST OUTSIDE OF TORONTO. HAMMOND HAS CREATED ARTWORK FOR EVERYTHING FROM FANTASY AND COMIC-BOOK ART TO CHILDREN'S MAGAZINES, POSTERS, AND BOOK ILLUSTRATION.

RICHARD CARBAJAL HAS A BROAD SPECTRUM OF ILLUSTRATIVE SPECIALTIES. HIS BACKGROUND HAS FOCUSED ON LARGE-SCALE INSTALLATIONS AND SCENERY. CARBAJAL RECENTLY HAS EXPANDED INTO THE BOOK PUBLISHING AND ADVERTISING MARKETS.

Text copyright © 2011 by Lerner Publishing Group, Inc.
Illustrations © 2011 by Lerner Publishing Group, Inc.

Graphic Universe™ is a trademark of Lerner Publishing Group, Inc.

All rights reserved. International copyright secured. No part of this book may be reproduced, stored in a retrieval system, or transmitted in any form or by any means—electronic, mechanical, photocopying, recording, or otherwise—without the prior written permission of Lerner Publishing Group, Inc., except for the inclusion of brief quotations in an acknowledged review.

Graphic Universe™
A division of Lerner Publishing Group, Inc.
241 First Avenue North
Minneapolis, MN 55401 U.S.A.

Website address: www.lernerbooks.com

Littlefield, Holly, 1963–
        The rooftop adventure of Minnie and Tessa, factory fire survivors / by Holly Littlefield ; adapted by Amanda Doering Tourville ; illustrated by Ted Hammond ; illustrated by Richard Carbajal.
        p.   cm. — (History's kid heroes)
        Summary: Two immigrant friends, Jewish Minnie and Catholic Tessa, work long hours at New York City's Triangle Shirtwaist Factory, and when a fire breaks out on March 25, 1911, trapping dozens of workers inside, they help one to escape the flames. Includes facts about the factory, the fire, and its aftermath.
        Includes bibliographical references.
        ISBN: 978-0-7613-6179-4 (lib. bdg. : alk. paper)
        1. Triangle Shirtwaist Company—Fire, 1911—Juvenile fiction. 2. Graphic novels. [1. Graphic novels. 2. Triangle Shirtwaist Company—Fire, 1911—Fiction. 3. Immigrants—Fiction. 4. Catholics—Fiction. 5. Jews—United States—Fiction. 6. New York (N.Y.)—History—1898–1951—Fiction.]
I. Tourville, Amanda Doering, 1980– II. Hammond, Ted, ill. III. Carbajal, Richard, ill. IV. Title.
PZ7.7.L58Roo 2011
974.7'041—dc22   2010028952

Manufactured in the United States of America
1—CG—12/31/10